THE INN AT
THE END
OF THE WORLD

Fourteen Tales for the Imagination

Dan Hamilton

NUMINOUS PRESS

ISBN 978-0-9794841-5-5

Numinous Press
numinouspress@sbcglobal.net

1 2 3 4 5 6 7 8 9 10

This collection is for all the friends
who heard and read and encouraged
in what was otherwise a difficult decade
(1971-1980)

Keith Anderson
(and the rest from Rose-Hulman)

Carol Hunt Loveless
(and the rest from Evansville)

Irene Chilcote Wagley

Colleen Somar Wright

Ron and Barb Knuckles

Concrete and the Sea is for Delaine Peffley,
who became a full citizen of the City in 1979

BY DAN HAMILTON

Forgiveness

Tales of the Forgotten God:
  The Beggar King
  The Chameleon Lady
  The Everlasting Child

EDITED BY DAN HAMILTON

George MacDonald Novels -
  The Parish Papers:
    A Quiet Neighborhood
    The Seaboard Parish
    The Vicar's Daughter
  The Last Castle
  The Prodigal Apprentice
  On Tangled Paths
  The Elect Lady
  Home Again
  The Boyhood of Ranald Bannerman
  The Genius of Willie MacMichael
  The Wanderings of Clare Skymer

WITH ELIZABETH HAMILTON

Should I Home School?
Look Both Ways

WITH DR. EDWIN W. BROWN

In Pursuit of C. S. Lewis

THE INN AT THE END OF THE WORLD

Dan Hamilton

foreword ~ 1

prologue:
THE LAST OF THE WINE ~ 4

then:
A CURE FOR UNICORN ~ 8
SHADOWBOX ~ 19

now:
CAPTAIN SUNSHINE AND THE RIGHT BROTHERS ~ 31
HENDERSON'S LION ~ 35
CONCRETE AND THE SEA ~ 39
THE LADY AND THE TIGER ~ 41

someday:
THROUGH THE GLASS DARKLY ~ 47
FOOLS' FOREST ~ 54
THE TREASURE OF GALLOWS HOUSE ~ 76

elsewhere:
THE FATE OF THE MOOR-WITCH ~ 89
TEETH IN THE NIGHT ~ 94
THE WHEEL OF THE SKY ~ 99

epilogue:
A CHILD OF THE SNOWS ~ 117
THE INN AT THE END OF THE WORLD ~ 118

afterword ~ 147

foreword

Those who have read *Tales of the Forgotten God (The Beggar King*, *The Chameleon Lady*, and *The Everlasting Child)* may want to know how the tales in this collection relate to the trilogy.

Comparisons are inevitable. They are also justified.

For the most part, the separate stories here were written prior to the publication of *The Beggar King* and even well before the planning and writing of *The Chameleon Lady* and *The Everlasting Child*.

Back in the previous millennium, this book was submitted to InterVarsity Press as a collection of short stories called *After the Rain*. My editor, Cindy Bunch, liked the book but doubted the corporate interest in marketing short fantasy. She and Andy Le Peau suggested that I extract five related stories about a wandering beggar and expand them into a full-length novel. "And while you're at it," they requested, "could you write two sequels? Calvin Miller's *Singer* books did very well for us as a fantasy trilogy, and we'd like to continue the tradition."

I swallowed hard, said "Of course!" - and began the two-year quest to build a complete trilogy on the sparse foundation of those few separate tales.

Those five stories originally included with this collection formed the basis for the chapters of the same name in *The Beggar King*:

"The Dead of Night"
"After the Rain"
"Trial by Fire"
"Before Winter"
"Beauty and the Feast"

After these pieces were removed and rewoven into the trilogy, the remaining tales began to take on different shapes and lean in different directions, and I found they would not go away. Even while working on other projects, I kept returning to this odd collection in equally odd moments - and eventually completed them over the next twenty years.

Is this collection, then, a prequel or sequel to the *Forgotten God* trilogy? No - though in many ways it forms a companion volume to it. It is both different from *Forgotten God* and yet subtly familiar. In mathematical terms, the geometry of the two universes is congruent but not identical. Some views (and even names) are common, and some of the expressions and explorations of possibilities are very similar.

The settings may be vaguely in the past, the present, the future, and even somewhere else outside of the timestream we know. The Elder God appears here frequently - though not always by that name. Here also is the original appearance of the Child, though in a much different role than that later developed in the trilogy. Hints of the City are also present throughout. There is no Covenant the Beggar in these pages, though there are one or two figures who do similar work.

Nor are these stories internally connected, except -

- the first and the last, which are bridged by Chesterton's powerful, haunting poem, and

- the three stories in the *someday* section.

Further notes appear in the afterword.

This book was not written in a single moment; my children were not even born when I began recording these tales, and now they are adults and well-suited to appreciate that some good things take time. Nor is this collection intended to be read in a single sitting; I think it best suited to be savored slowly over multiple nights with abundant time for reflection in between.

Look carefully; in these worlds, not everything is what it first appears to be. Fantasy on the surface; Biblical truths at the very core; fuel from and for the imagination from beginning to end.

Dan Hamilton
Indianapolis, Indiana
November 1, 2016

prologue:

THE LAST OF THE WINE

THE LAST OF THE WINE

"By the gods, after all these years - and now it's time. Anger? Or sadness? I cannot choose." Jupiter played with a piece of drifting cloud as he spoke.

Saturn's reply rolled like low thunder. "Should there not be relief? We have never been great enough for all the glory our worshipers laid upon our shoulders."

All the gods knew that burden as they rode the night clouds above the sleeping earth. They had all come at the unspoken summons - had come without question and assembled without fanfare.

Neptune, misted and dripping, paced restlessly. Rain fell in the Mediterranean, miles below.

Pluto tended the great hazy fire in their midst. Sparks sizzled unheeded against his skin.

Venus, gazing across that fire, shivered at the red-eyed shadows beyond. Not all the gods were both beautiful and good.

Some rested, listening to their names in scattered late-night-worship phrases rising from the darkened planet. Prayers wheeled past, sparkling comets, trailing words like *immortal* and *eternal* sad and ironic in their wake. "O darker truth than that!" offered one of the reclining gods, to no one in particular. "Creators? We are the created. Forged by those who have mortality thrust upon them. Eternal? Eternally vulnerable, rather, and when there are no more believers we will cease to be. We will fade with the scattering smoke of that final sacrifice, and the forgetfulness that follows honor."

"We are spared that," said another. "Now the end comes another way."

The fire flared on new timber, warming the backs of two who sprawled at the cloud's feathered edge and gazed upward at the spiraling galaxies.

Bacchus offered his flask. "How do you feel, my friend? We have not talked together for many tedious turnings."

Mars drank deeply of both the wine and the night air. "Weak, longing, and weary. I always envied you - men feed me on their hatred, and you on their pleasure. He who serves me does so from fear and corruption and not good desire. They tire so quickly of wars, because there are so many, but they always find occasion to seek the flavor of the vine."

"Perhaps. But they present you the purity of passion, flinging me only the fleeting fruits of forgetfulness and the doting of drooling drunkards." He squeezed his hands together in the air, and dark wine trickled weakly from his clenched fingers into the empty flask. "The wine wanes. My hands hold hollowness. But feast, my friend - drink the dregs. It is the last of the old wine - and the finest."

"Let us drink, then, to the new wine that comes after."

"To the new wine." They savored their salute in silence.

Mercury wandered closer to the fire, and Pluto called to him over his shoulder. "Ah, messenger. You stood long on the edge looking out. What did you see? Hear? Fathom? What final words do you bear us?"

"I have seen only enough to know that this night will not be forgotten. The gulf of time opened before me, and I saw a man who bent to mark an epitaph for the old gods. I heard the words he began to choose - he wrote of the night when the gods assembled and all the tickings of time were divided. All that has led to this night men will call Before - and all that follows will bear the name of After."

"And what comes After?"

"I do not know. I saw also a giant, and a child - far away, speaking across a fire, and the man wrote the words that came from their mouths. Then the vision was veiled, and I could not total the sum of their words. The oracle is incomplete: a story with an ending we shall never know. Time has two sides now, and blind are we who see only the half."

The fire crackled. Pluto tended its hunger. "Perhaps your shrouded message is only just. We have long dwelt as shadows, shadows under a shadow of ignorance. Naming me the Lord of the Underworld, men besought me for favor and mercy and deliverance. Broken they were when we met in their passing, when they beheld the frailness of my true stature and saw the weakness of my power. They were torn with terror as they turned to face the bright darkness alone."

"It is good that we have no souls. Perhaps a kinder fate awaits us." Pluto poked the fire again. There was no more fuel to burn.

One by one, the waiting gods drifted to join him around the flicker of the waning flames. Venus quietly took Psyche's hand in hers. The motion spread, and soon they all stood linked in great circles about the glowing embers.

The coals winked out with a whisper of release. The clouds rode suddenly stark and empty in the moonlight.

And a star bloomed over Bethlehem.

###

then:

A CURE FOR UNICORN

SHADOWBOX

A CURE FOR UNICORN

~ one ~

Maheera slept restlessly in her cottage at the edge of the forest. Then *he* passed near the cottage, moving silently, and she woke and knew the unicorn had at last come to the land.

He withdrew then, though not far away, and Maheera could no longer feel him so strongly. She waited for the first faint glimmer of dawn, then made her way to the village and across the still-empty open square to a small dwelling. She rapped gently against the wooden doorframe, and then entered. An old woman already standing before the fire turned to her and beckoned the young woman to join her close to the flames.

"You are abroad early, Maheera," said the old woman. "Most dreamers are only beginning their sleep when the sun is beginning his work."

"Mother Ramah? Please tell me again about the unicorns."

"Will you never tire of hearing? Of course I shall tell you again." They took seats near the fire - easily, like old friends accustomed to their places. "The unicorns were born where the sun quenches its fire every evening, where white ice quiets the seas that lie at the edge of the world. Born, yes, but not mortal, coming and going like the frost that fathered them, burning great and flaring with ceaseless fire like the sun that was their mother. They were born for the dance, and to bring delight, and the Lord of the Unicorns - the Son of the Elder God - sent them forth to bring joy with their dancing, to seek out the untouched maidens who waited for them in hope and longing.

"And so they did, for time without measure, to generation upon generation, until that day in a bygone age, when both men and women knew things that were better left unknown, when unrighteous power and dark secrets were made manifest and practiced openly.

"There was a woman then who coveted the unicorn, who beheld its beauty but was neither softened nor gladdened by it. Yes, she hated it, for she was young and foolish and exceedingly pretty, but proud and jealous and vain and vexing. Most held her to be a spell-thrower - none thought her a virgin. In her own village the unicorn spurned her in the sight of all, and chose a maiden less fair, to dance with her and bring her honor. And the anger of the jealous woman burned hot, and she called upon the powers beneath her feet to cast a double curse. 'From this day on, every unicorn, every one of your kind, shall bring heartbreak as well as joy; and every maiden who dances with you shall long for you and never be satisfied again, and her world shall be empty for her because she has known and lost that joy!' And when she had cursed his entire race, she uttered a malediction upon him, and turned him into a mortal man. Then she called down clouds of fog and escaped, and was never seen again.

"The unicorn - a man now, tall, golden, fair, and handsome - was consoled in his grief by the maiden who had danced with him, and no one knows in certain truth what happened to them after that.

"And since then, through two hand's worth of generations, where have the unicorns gone? Some say that they have all passed from the land, not in death but in sorrow. And perhaps they have passed on to a land that deserves them more, a land that meets them not with hatred ...

"Some say that the unicorns yet come, but secretly, not openly as in past days. And a few yet believe - a few give heed to the rumors - a few have kept themselves pure for that hour of joy which is its own devastation."

Having listened carefully, Maheera just as carefully asked a question. "Mother ... have *you* ever seen the unicorn? Do *you* believe?"

Ramah paused for a long moment and stirred the fire. "You have never asked me that, and I have long held my breath in fear for the day when you did. I will tell you a story first, and then I will answer you.

"There was an old woman who was old to me when I was young. She it was who taught me all I know, though it was many years before I would listen fully to her words. I asked her many things, to test her and tease her, then I disbelieved or disregarded her answers.

"But one day I asked her of the unicorn, and she told me that which I have told you. I did not believe her then, either - I scorned her and asked her how she knew these things - was she so old that she had seen these things herself? She seemed very sad, then, and showed me an old leather book with ancient writings from many hands - a store of wisdom that is the memory of the years. She showed me the story of the unicorn - very near the front of the book it was, for it is an old tale.

"She said that not all the words in the Wisdom - for so she called it - could be tested for their truth, but she had tested many, and found them all true.

"Then she marked for me a page in the middle of the Wisdom, neither very old nor very recent. They were words about the Old Laws of the Elder God, which He laid down with the foundation of the world. The Old Laws foresaw that men would bring banes, spells, and evil curses upon the earth, and would certainly destroy it unless they were restrained by a higher and greater and purer power. So the Old Laws are written to govern even the foulest banes: they provide, in the words of the Wisdom, that every curse which is laid will contain the seed of its own cure."

Ramah rose and took a leather-wrapped book from a closed cupboard near the mantle, then continued. "I have puzzled over those words for many long years now, for the Wisdom passed to me as she wished it to. She was, as I am now, a mother of none with many daughters. I received it with pleasure, and have it still - and I will show you the words she marked for me that day."

The writing was faded and small and curious, and Maheera could scarcely decipher the letters. "There is," it said, "a Cure for Unicorn. My own daughter has danced with the unicorn. Then for three days she was torn and alone, bearing the weight of the curse, and I her own father was helpless and without balm. On the third day her rescue came - the rescue that was born of the first bane. Blessed is she now, for her second glory is greater than her first." Then the words that followed went on to other things.

"But what do these words mean?" Maheera asked. "What is the cure?"

"I do not know. The writer used too few words and said too little to mean too much."

Maheera turned the words over and over in her mind, but found more wonder than comfort in them. And she returned at last to an old question. "But have *you* seen the unicorn?"

Ramah smiled, though there was pain as well as pleasure behind the smile. "I have. I told you that I did not believe the tales, or the Wisdom, until after I was grown. And I came to believe the unicorn first, and then because of the unicorn I came to believe other things.

"He came to me in the woods, the very day that the Wisdom passed into my hands. I was walking there alone, mourning my friend, mourning my own loss in not loving her sooner and better, and suddenly *he* was before me - standing silently, calmly but with great power, like a god come terribly to life. He was there only for a thundering heartbeat - too short that I should do anything but stare and fear and worship, too long that I should ever ever forget. And then he was gone - and I listened to his hooves beating the ground like hammers, fading away into a distance I could never hope to enter."

She poked the fire again before continuing. "Perhaps he revealed himself to me both as a rebuke and a reward. A reward for believing, at long last, and a rebuke for having waited so long to believe. Or perhaps it was that I could not have seen him before - for some things must be believed to be seen.

"He did not dance with me, but he favored me with a sight of him, and with a warming blast of breath upon my face. He did not dance with me, for when I was young I did not believe, and when I believed I was no longer young.

"Ever since that day I have kept the Wisdom safe, and read it, and believed it, and waited for him to return, in some form or fashion.

"Before this day I have not told you all I know, nor all that I have seen. I have not wished to encourage you or make you bold to go where only the foolish and the very brave go. But some men - and many women - will not be discouraged at any cost. Do you still stand among them?"

Maheera nodded, a sudden heat showing behind her eyes.

"Are not the men of this village - or the next - enough for you?" asked Ramah.

The heat spilled over into a sudden torrent of words. "So they would have me believe - but I sent them all away. They are all tame. They have lost that which would enable them still to roam the forest and dance in the moonlight. They have ceased to have anything of the child or of the true wildness about them. I mean the wildness of the man who revels in the beauty of the forest, and not the wildness of a man who cares nothing for that beauty. The men who have sought my hand would rather stalk and slay the deer than run with it. Now they hunt in the light of the moon and do not simply pleasure in it. They no longer race through the meadows for the joy of going swiftly. They have forgotten how to laugh. They are old, even though they are young."

Maheera leaned forward on her hands, and her voice grew softer. "They are not evil - so I may not condemn them. They are courteous, attentive, even protective ... but can any of them satisfy me now? How can I be content with them? Perhaps other men exist who are not like these, but I do not know where they are. Do I truly risk much by seeking another with a heart like mine - even if I am his and he is mine only for a day?"

Ramah had no answer, but only offered a last caution. "Count first the cost, and beware the heartbreak, for both will surely be yours - for the curse is not ended, even if a cure lies somewhere in the land. And after *him* how can any man ever lift your heart so high again?"

With her eyes closed against the brightness of the fire, Maheera said slowly, "I know the peril, and I have reckoned the price. And I have not so very far to seek." She opened her eyes. "He is here already. I felt him moving in the forest this morning when I awoke. I am only waiting for him to call me, for I know he came for me. Do not ask me to tell you how I know."

"I knew that you knew, and I need no explanation. The deep well of a woman's heart is not to be plumbed by the sort of knowledge that can be justified. I did not feel him, for he did not come for me, but I dreamed of him last night, and so guessed at the rest. He *would* come for *you*, for who else has believed in him and waited for him, kept herself pure for him and longed to behold him? Even though I think of him, never have I been able to dream of him. Yet last night he pranced in my dreams, unbidden, and I knew it as a sign. And so I rose and built a fire and waited for you to come.

"When he comes to you, Maheera, chase him with that which cannot catch him, and bind him with that which cannot hold him. Pursue him slowly, and with desire, and know that your ecstasy and his will be as much in the chase as in the dance that follows after. Follow him with praise, and laughter, and match his gait as he matches yours, and you will run with the pace of poetry and the speed of the sunshine. Go with my blessing. Perhaps he waits for you even now."

Maheera rose and reluctantly returned the Wisdom.

Ramah smiled, and said, "I see it draws you already. Some day it will be yours, and *you* will have to unravel the other puzzles and the promises inside." Maheera turned to the door, and Ramah called gently after her, "Please - return to me after ... after. I, who have glimpsed him once, should like to see him again through your eyes."

She nodded, nearly weeping, and left.

~ two ~

At noon, while Maheera was drawing water, *he* came to her, masculine and powerful, shining, serene, and stood beneath the shadowed trees across the meadow. His glory smote her heart, and she threw her bucket aside unheeded and splashed through the stream and ran across the field into the cool forest, laughing, longing, chasing, desiring the dance that only he might grant her ...

~ three ~

Stars reigned over the village when Maheera returned. The fire still glowed before Ramah as she turned the pages of the Wisdom, musing over the legends and waiting for the daughter who both was and was not her own.

Maheera entered without a word, and only huddled near the fire and stared for many slow minutes into the flames. The tracks of recent tears glowed on her face, while her hair tangled within itself and held captive a host of leaves and fresh flower petals. Her face was flushed, reverent, like one who had been awed, gentled, subdued, exalted, and ravished all in one long moment. Then she spoke, in a husky voice, without looking away from the fire, "He came! At noon."

"And?"

"And I chased him with spider thread and weaver's down, and with songs of children, and he chose to catch me, and to let me dance with him in the far meadows and then to ride him ... did I mount him myself or did he run beneath me? I clung to him bareback and we plunged into the heart of the forest and sped long under the trees and sometimes above them and always under the sun and the stars ... and we danced again, and his hooves were like gold and his mane flew like white storm clouds and his tail was like a silver streamer in the wind ... and when the sun was gone I lay breathless on the grass and watched him rear over me and then he touched my heart with his golden horn and then he was gone like the wind in the grass ...

"So now I am here. I don't know how I came back, or from where. I don't remember. But he is gone. That is all I can think of. He brought me all the joy I ever knew or hoped to find, and now he has carried it all away with him." She started to weep again.

The old woman waited a few moments. "And do you now regret your choice - or your chase?"

She looked up quickly. "No! I would run to him again, were it somehow still this morning and the deed not yet done. It is simply ... so cold now. So lonely."

"I have no wonder at that. You have been ravished by a love that is not mortal. And now your heart has a fresh hollow that cannot easily be filled."

"But he ... he *spoke* to me as he turned to go. Like the breeze whispering. 'Maheera, my beloved. I will not leave you desolate. Wait for the one I send, who comes for you, who travels in my name and speaks to you with my voice. The Old Laws are ever true.' And that was all."

"And so you are not forsaken."

"So I must trust. But who is this one who is to come?"

"I do not know. But there *are* unicorns, and one *did* come to you as in elder days, so the Lord of the Unicorns must yet live and hold power. And if a cure for unicorn exists, then can you say that He who sends them will deny you your heartsease? And we have the words of the writer in the Wisdom. Remember that he said the cure was as real as the curse - and have not all the other words proven true?"

~ four ~

Ramah sat beside her door, continually sifting the sounds that floated past her on the twilight air. She had listened and watched in hope - but for what she scarcely knew - each one of the three evenings since Maheera had danced with the unicorn.

Then the wind brought the faintest snatch of noise - hoofbeats a long way out along the road that came from over the hills - hoofbeats that thundered softly, drew nearer, and stopped somewhere just out of sight of the village. There was silence, then, and what might have been a horse's warm whicker, and then the hooves pounded away over the hills again, and Ramah's heart pounded with them, for the sound of the hooves had been both faintly strange and even more faintly familiar.

Then nothing for many moments, and then the soft footsteps of someone approaching through the trees. Then a stranger emerged from the gloom before her, stopped in front of her, and bowed. He was a young man, and striking - hair the color of fresh snow dusted with purest gold, eyes brown like the earth and deep and piercing. He towered over her like a sturdy tree, and he carried the sweet loamy smell of old leaves and forest moss and hidden green places. His gaze burrowed straight into Ramah's as he spoke.

"You hold the Wisdom here?" Untamed power underlaid his voice, like strong currents beneath a calm sea, and his words were less a question than a statement.

"I do," she answered, awed but reassured. "Whom do you seek?"

"I seek the maiden who was favored by the Unicorn."

"And you ...?"

"I am the seed of the Unicorn. He himself brought me here - from far away, past many villages, over many miles. And I am also the comfort of the Unicorn, sent to the one who was wounded by the Dance."

"*We* have been waiting ... though we did not know for what - or whom - we waited. She is here, and has need of you. Come - I will lead you to her." They walked away together, and the old woman wondered at the white-golden shaggy hair and quiet litheness and muscled grace of the stranger. They stopped before Maheera's cottage, and Ramah motioned forward with her hand. "She is here."

The stranger called for Maheera, gently, and entered. The old woman heard her cry out, and after that came the sound of tears that have their root in sudden joy.

Ramah walked away quietly, knowing that some magic is for two hearts alone. But very late that night she sat unnoticed beneath a tree and watched the two dancing together in the meadows under the moon.

Their pleasure brought her delight and sadness mingled, for her own unicorn-ache returned to haunt her - that wound, though not soul-deep, she had suffered in a single moment in the woods so many years gone. She whispered her sorrow into the darkness, seeking comfort from the shadows under the trees. Then she cradled her head in her arms upon her knees, and wept.

How much time passed she did not know, but the moon had fallen far down the sky when she felt a presence behind her. A deeper shadow than the shadow of the forest fell over her, and she knew without moving that she, too, had been honored, and not forsaken. She turned, quietly, and the holy vision was there.

What happened after that she would never fully reveal, saying only to Maheera the next day, "It was not a dance ... it was less than that, but still high, and far greater than I had right to hope or receive. Though we did not dance, I yet touched him, and now I know glory."

They were silent for a long while, and watched Maheera's comforter chopping wood where once the unicorn had bloomed.

"Did he leave you with only that?" asked Maheera. "No word? No blessing?"

"He left me himself - in my dreams. He told me, as he left me, that I would behold him always in my sleep. A small gift, perhaps, to some - yet healing, and a great solace to this old heart."

~ five ~

Maheera's firstborn was a boy, broad-shouldered, blond, and fair - and so were the second, and the three after that. They had two mothers, for Ramah came often and watched them grow merry and glorious in the image and company of their father. She also watched as many who had daughters came seeking the arrangement of marriages, and she watched as all were turned away.

And the two exalted women, who had received the secret honors, spoke often together of the things they treasured in their hearts.

"They have their father's blood," said Maheera, "and he his, and pure runs the strain to the one who first suffered the curse. No one will ever tame them, nor is it mine to grant them to women who have not yet learned to believe. They are set aside for the women who will one day dance with the Unicorn. As my husband was sent to me, to fill my ceaseless hunger, to quench my deepest thirsts, so shall my sons be sent. I will not send them, nor will my husband. The Unicorn himself will come and call them and bear them away. The joy they bring will never grow old, never fade, never ache."

She turned her eyes to Ramah, and then to the nearby edge of the forest. "Even yet, when the moon is bright and the wind warm from the south, or the snow is crisp and unbroken, we two go to dance on the roof of the meadows or under the high beams of the forest." She gazed long at her old friend, with a wonder that would never quite fade away. "The words of the Wisdom are true. A Cure for Unicorn. The Old Laws will not be broken."

###

SHADOWBOX

~ one ~

A dry squeal like old coffins opening pierced the night and woke the whole village in sudden streams of icy sweat. A dark wagon, laden with small black boxes, passed with unquiet wheels through the streets and stopped in the center of the village square. Illuminated only by the moon, a tall man in ebony clothing stepped down from the cart and hobbled the horse that was the color of old midnights. He stood in the square and lifted up his voice and his arms. The people watched from darkened doorways and unlit windows, trembling, yet they came at his command under the spell of power, and they filled the square with their silent presence. Fear lay heavy on them - fear, and the fear of fear itself. They looked everywhere but at the man and at the miniature boxes lying like dark caskets on the wagon bed.

He spoke. "I am the Master of the Shadows. Among men I bear the name of Shadowhawk - you have heard of me from of old." He leered, and the moon was veiled by sudden clouds. "I have come to make with each of you an agreement - a transaction of fair exchange. I have that which you value. You have that which I have long desired.

"You have each been burdened with a name, and your soul has been bent to match that name. All along your earthbound path your soul, passing, has cast its dark shadows and left them behind. Behind - dead - withered - forgotten - abandoned - cleansed by time of all that made them hateful. Or so you thought - until tonight. I tell you again that I am the Master of the Shadows - and who but their master should know their lairs and their secret places? They were hidden, but undead, undying, until I walked nameless paths and called them forth - called them, found them, sorted them, and kept them ...

"And where should I keep such sad and shameful secrets but in shadowboxes?" He brandished a tiny coffin from the cart. "For each of you a casket, your name in guilty gilded letters. Name - soul - shadow - shadowbox - name again. The circle is complete.

"Yet you might break that circle - if you could silence those dark images ... and I could hand them to you, tidy bundles, box by box, name by name, and you could take them away and bury them. But then again, I have the power to stand in this square and call your name and open the box - to release for all to see your stale lusts, long hidden - your forgotten envies - your haunted diversions - your ghastly recollections.

"Hear me, fools, and tremble, for that is what I have come here to do - and all the earth will know your deepest secrets. Your own shame will accuse you and smother you and fill your empty soul and sicken you unto death. You shall never recover from it. Your accumulated sins shall mark you and scar you and be a sign for all until you seek refuge in your grave.

"All this I shall do, and bring you to ruin and despair, here, tomorrow twilight before all assembled, unless ... unless ..." He broke off his words and brandished a handful of scrolled parchments. "A simple trade, an exchange, a barter. Sign this, each one of you who would keep your footsteps buried, and I shall pass over your shame tomorrow and leave your shadowbox unopened on my cart. Come - take a scroll, and depart - I have nothing to add to my words. Your choices are clear."

They came in horrified silence and took their parchments in trembling hands. The last to come was an old and weathered man whose true name all the village had forgotten, an odd man with more unsettling questions than comforting answers, a man called by the villagers simply Seeker.

~ two ~

The moon had long gone before Seeker, sleepless like all the rest, roused himself from his fearful stupor and fed more fuel to the fire, hoping in vain that the light and warmth would drive his fears back into the shadows. He finally lit a candle and dared to open the scroll and read there the bargain offered him. He began, but did not finish; the beginning was horrid enough, demanding that which Seeker had feared - a price of blood, and worse.

He laid his head upon the table and wept. He could not escape - either way the chains of his own past would drag him down to his death.

A knock at the door roused him. He opened it slowly against the night to find a stranger on his step. The stranger without entered without invitation, without word, but once he had crossed the threshold Seeker stood without fear. There was a faint, lingering, nearly-forgotten scent about the stranger, as though he carried balm somewhere deep within the folds of his clothes.

"How is it that I know you?" Seeker asked. "You stand familiar to me, but I have never seen you before."

"No? Perhaps not. But then again perhaps. For now, call me Stranger." Then he laughed - and his laugh woke beautiful aching echoes in the house. The sweet smell grew stronger.

"Please," Seeker said. "Laugh again. For that moment, just that blessed moment, your laughter was like solid rock and this accursed night like defiled sand that is washed away by the tide."

"Yes. I shall laugh again - and you shall join me. But that time is not now." He looked at Seeker's table and the parchment. "An old man sleepless before the dawn, and the remains of a fire that was kindled in the depths of the night. Your past weighs you down."

Seeker hung his head. "Yes. All my life - all these weary years - I have sought to shed my shadows, or slay them, or redeem them, and now the very shame I have dreaded draws near - nearer - to fall on me tomorrow."

"I know." Stranger smiled. "And what do you intend to do with this?" He pointed to the parchment. "It has the look of a decision that will not wait."

"I have already decided. The night is chill - let us have at least a blessing of warmth from this curse." He hurled it on the fire and they watched the flames transform it to ashes. "Do you know this Shadowhawk?"

"I do."

"Does he bear us truth? Do the shadows lie waiting at his command? Will he loose them upon us?"

"He is a liar by heart, though he tells the truth when it benefits him. His power is real, though limited, and his threats are not always made idly. You have heard his threat, and yet you burned the scroll. And the whole world will see your shadows tomorrow. Does it not frighten you? Horrify you?"

"Yes. And more than that." He buried his face in his hands. "It will kill me. But rather that than the bondage of my soul."

"Even that is a hollow victory."

"I know. When I die my shadows will be my shroud."

Stranger took him by the arm and led him out into the street. "Perhaps there is no escape to be purchased, but then perhaps rescue already walks among you. You are a brave man - and a wise one. But not wise enough. Come - let your bravery bring you new wisdom, and the fulfillment of that which you have dared to hope all your life."

"Why do I trust you? You are Stranger to me."

"Yes - but not you to me. Already I call you friend, and soon you will call me Friend." He guided their steps through the stricken town to an old building standing mute and forlorn. Stranger opened the great double doors against the protest of unused hinges.

Seeker lingered at the door after Stranger had entered. "Here? This is an ancient temple. There is nothing here but dust and darkness."

Stranger drew him inside. "You have only the memory of a man. Once glory dwelt here, and there was sunshine instead of shadows, devotion instead of dust, supplication instead of silence." He led them through the empty outer chambers and mounted the steps to the altar. Light began to shine from somewhere, and soft colors came to play on the walls. "All memory of me is lost in the land - this temple lies deserted, and none are left to teach those who have the heart to learn. That is why the black stealer of souls has come - but there are other, older reasons for his coming that even he does not suspect. And for the same reasons I myself have returned." He lifted his arms and light flared sharply from every corner, as though a thousand suns had risen along the walls. He waved his arms, and the deep dust vanished. "He comes to this town in darkness, because his deeds and theirs are dark; I have come to this town in secret, bringing light, because I have known the deeds of your lives and the needs of your hearts. Come, Seeker, approach the altar - it is time that your shadows died at my hands. Power is before you, and if you turn away there is no other strength to aid you."

Seeker came, and knelt. "What shall I offer you? For this is an altar, and demands sacrifice."

"I seek your heart, that it may be broken here. Broken, but not sacrificed. I shall provide that. It is hard, but I will help you - behold that which I put before your eyes."

Seeker stared at the flat top of the altar as, like a tiny drama, he saw a single moment from his youth frozen in figures there, and the figures began to move, and the figure that had been Seeker spoke and drew back its arm, and Seeker knew what would happen and so turned away.

"No, Seeker, do not turn away. There will be shame - but here and now, alone with me. And if not here, then tomorrow before the multitude. You know what Shadowhawk will do with what he has collected - see now what I will do with all that you surrender to me. Behold your shadows, and do not fall back from them." He placed his hands on Seeker's trembling head. "You must either cover them with light, or they will drown you in darkness. I will show them to you - you must see them, remember them, name them, admit them as your own and then surrender them to me. It will tear you, but you will not die, and I shall not leave your side."

The haunted drama began. For each scene of each act Seeker choked back his shame and named the darkness his own and gave it over into the waiting patient hands. And Stranger took each shadow and crushed it into a ball. Razor edges slashed his hands, and blood soaked into the crumpled mass and dripped onto the altar.

Seeker wept, and his tears streamed unabated until the final curtain was allowed to fall. Only then did Seeker look beyond the altar and beyond the hands to the face, and only then did he see that Stranger wept also.

The mass of old sharp shadows lay crumpled into smooth stone on Stranger's palm. His blood had stained the blackness red, and as Seeker watched even the red faded and white incandescence took its place. The flare of purity dazzled him and outshone even the sourceless brilliance from the temple walls.

Seeker bowed his head. "*Thank you* does not say enough," he said. "You have done all that was needed, and more than I dared hope for. The shadows are gone. But what can I offer you in return that will not insult you? I have no money, no fame, no secret treasure. And you cannot be repaid with words."

"Then repay me with your actions now - and only later with your words. They may hold more treasure than you perceive. But now, call me Friend and not Stranger, for I have redeemed you."

"I will dare to call you Friend if you bid me."

"I ask no treasure from you but yourself. Come to me, come with me, come do my bidding, and we two shall stand alone against Shadowhawk - and against another who shall soon arrive at his bidding. Tonight I give you power, for tomorrow you shall need it." He paused. "You were given a name which passed from memory when the town called you Seeker, and now both names are dead with your shadows. I name you Finder, for you have found that which you have long sought. But let that be a name for others to use in their dealing with you. It is my heart's desire to give you a name not known on earth."

And Friend called him by a new name, and Finder's heart leaped within him at the sound, for he knew it to be a truer name, truest, higher, a name that could never decay, never fade, never tarnish.

"Behold!" Friend held out his hand, and turned the white stone over in his palm, and the letters of the new name were graven in marks of fire on the stone. Then Friend taught Finder his own name - a name of power to call down against Shadowhawk on the morrow. Finder did not repeat the name; he would never forget it, and it was no name to be uttered lightly. It was a solid name, and the syllables rang with righteousness like steel on stone.

"Blessed are you, Finder, among men, for not many desire your knowledge - yet - and still fewer men would have willingly paid the price you offered this night. You have received the highest gift already - but I have another gift for you." He led the way to an inner door whose lock was shrouded in cobweb and layered with the dust of years. Friend opened it with a quiet word, and Finder stepped awestruck into the room behind. Spines of worn leather looked down from the rows of shelves, and the smell of old parchments swirled around him.

Friend gestured about the room. "Despise not the old things. Here is Truth, and it changes not. Abide here, and study - as, indeed, you would have done could you have found this room before." He reached out and touched the old man's eyes. "I have taken your blindness from you - blindness you knew not that you carried. And I have opened your mind, because your heart was open first. Wisdom awaits you - the wisdom of men long gone who have walked these same narrow paths. All this has been kept for ones such as you - protected, made safe from fools and vandals. Heed not the passing of the hours, for sleep shall not work its dreary magic upon you until the trials of this day are at an end."

He lit the ancient candles with a pinch of his fingers and left Finder alone in peace to do his task.

~ three ~

Reluctantly, dusk and the villagers gathered in the square to await Shadowhawk. And when he came he spoke no words to the multitude, but simply stood on the wagon and called the first name. The one who had been called trembled forward and surrendered the scroll he had signed. Shadowhawk examined the parchment. "You have purchased the final burial of your shadows. I accept your service." He laid the labeled casket and the scroll in the recesses of the wagon and called the next name.

Not until he came to the woman called The Rose did he encounter anything but the silent offering of a signed scroll. When her name was called, a murmur moved through the crowd and then perished under the gaze of Shadowhawk. The Rose was a woman of the streets, and the image of the bright flower had been given her in derision. Her name was a byword of laughter, her past an open darkness. No one doubted that she would sign. The doubt was simply that any one box could contain her shadows.

She stood unmoving, head bowed, her hands empty of any scroll. Shadowhawk called her name a second time before she lifted her face and spoke.

"I will not sign. I burned your scroll last night. Since it could not warm my heart I let it warm my body."

"Foolish woman! Do you not understand what I possess the power to unleash?" He held her shadowbox high over his head.

"I do. But rather that than bondage to you. I have been a slave in this village all my life - a prisoner of others' passions, a captive of those who hold out the gold of life in exchange for my favors. I have had enough of these 'agreements.' Do your deed - release the foulness. My share is known, and none will be surprised to see that which was not known. I shall leave this square tonight with my shame renewed, but I shall walk forth free of your chains." She lifted her head high with the last of her courage and awaited the onslaught of the shadows.

Shadowhawk shrugged his shoulders and, with eloquent silence, opened the box. Hinges creaked; then fog, deathly black in the twilight, oozed out and spread throughout the square. The mist carried with it the stench of Rose's shadows, the charnel smell of rotting passions and undead defiant deeds, the decaying odor of loveless liaisons and lingering lecheries. Festered fallings now so foul that even the passing breeze was infected.

All saw, all knew, and all recoiled in fascinated revulsion.

"Breathe deeply, woman of the red flower! Look long! Scarlet and black are your name and your deeds. They defy you, damn you, destroy you, darken this present hour and all that follows after! The rest of you - inhale, examine, consider her shame! She stands accused, her secrets bare, and none can defend or deliver or cleanse or take away! Go now, woman, and take your shame with you!"

When she left, the mist followed her slowly like rolling fog seeking the lowlands. The air slowly cleared in the square, but each one there remembered well. Any lingering thoughts of rebellion or defiance were quenched. From each trembling soul thereafter Shadowhawk collected a scroll and was appeased.

Until his list held but one name, and he called for tribute from Seeker.

Silence. Shadowhawk called again. The answer came boldly, with a shock like sudden lightning.

"Call me not Seeker, but Finder! For power and freedom have fallen upon me, power to withstand you and freedom to defy you!"

"You too are a fool," replied Shadowhawk calmly and coldly. "As I crushed and blackened the other one, so shall I destroy you!" He opened the last casket and turned it over in the air.

A single white radiant stone fell from the box, and a sweet fragrance swept the square. All present saw the marks of fire on the stone, but only Finder knew the letters and the meaning.

Shadowhawk reeled back as though the stone were a curse and its light a flame to his flesh. The crowd stirred, wondered, and murmured. Shadowhawk cried out, "Be still! There is evil work here, and by this shining you are deceived!"

Then Finder answered with the name of power. The square flared with light at his words, and the darkness that slowly returned after was less hateful than before. All fled in terror save Shadowhawk and Finder, and the one named Friend who stood at Finder's side.

The rage and terror faded from Shadowhawk's voice even as he spoke, and his words turned icy with hatred. "I should have known it was you again. A pretty finish, that - but too late! My triumph is secure! Behold!" And even as he pointed, a tall, pale rider entered the village on horseback and tapped quietly at each house where the people lay hidden and weeping. All heard his whispered invitation, and many accepted his offer in a final spasm of despair. When Death was done he rode to the square and stopped before Shadowhawk. Over his shoulder Death held a bag, swollen and writhing with many burdens, and he opened the bag that Shadowhawk might peep inside. They both began to giggle, then snort, and finally broke into loud cruel laughter, flaunting their catch before the two who watched from across the square. Then Shadowhawk mounted and they rode slowly away with the wagon of caskets, Death grinning in unrestrained, unrelieved evil, Shadowhawk waving his booty of scrolls obscenely in the air. The weight of their presence did not die away with the echoes of hooves and wheels.

Finder and Friend wept openly in each other's arms, and when their grief had abated they stood and stared along the road where the dark pair had gone. Finder gestured in the silence and said, "I do not understand all that I have seen. You are the one who lives in the temple, yet you did not lift your hand - I thought power dwelt with the gods. Why did you not prevent this?"

"I shall yet crush Shadowhawk, and destroy his henchman Death, but the hour for that is not yet at hand. There is a season for all things, and this is the season for us to follow in the troubled wake of the two who sow shadows and reap souls. This is the hour for you to prove your devotion. You alone sought me before you knew either me or your need for me. You were the first, and because you were the first your cost was lessened. Many ears are now ready to hear the words we have to say. You knew the fear of shame, and recoiled from its approach; these others know now the full horror and despair. But in me and at my hands they may find a cure for shame - that shame which left to itself knows no end - and a way to redeem that which has otherwise been signed away and sealed in blood ...

"Do you recall the written wisdom you read in the night?" Finder nodded. "You shall make use of it now, and be blessed for your searching heart. They have already heard the voice of Death, speaking despair, but you shall be for them the voice of Hope. You shall speak, and explain, and share wisdom, and prepare the way for the deeds I stand ready to perform. Be surprised at nothing. I dealt with you in one way, but I have in no way approached my limits."

"Yes. I am here. And I have waited all my life to be a servant to the Truth." He opened his arms wide. "Where shall we begin?"

"There is one who stands now but a heartbeat from the open door of the temple. Next to you, she is the one who has tasted freedom tonight. Not freedom from her past, but freedom from the grasp of the one who wields shadows. She has dared that which even you did not dare - to live as though your soul were glass and all your shadows plain.

"No names are given in vain. The rose is a holy flower, and she longs for someone to touch her, heal her, renew her that she might be not The Rose in scorn but Lady Rose in truth. And I have a gift for her, as I had for you - the object of the heart's desire." He extended his hand, and rose petals fluttered from his fingers. Flowered fragrance filled the air. "This perfume is sweet but strong, and all memory of the scent she wears now will fade under its power."

Shadows retreated from their path as they left the square to seek The Rose and the other helpless hearts hiding in the village.

###

now:

CAPTAIN SUNSHINE AND THE RIGHT BROTHERS

HENDERSON'S LION

CONCRETE AND THE SEA

THE LADY AND THE TIGER

CAPTAIN SUNSHINE AND
THE RIGHT BROTHERS

We had been stranded on the island for two full years before Captain Sunshine came along. That wasn't what he called himself but he was crazy so we gave him a better name.

But that was later.

It was Orbur's fault that we were on the island. Our plane had come down with a smash on the rocky top of the island while I was flying it (I'm Wilville) and Orbur was supposed to be the mechanic. Both engines died and he said it wasn't his fault but he knows it was and he should be thankful I made such a good landing on this forsaken piece of blasted rock.

The island has no beach just impossible cliffs and wild waves that pound high up on the rock. The sea is always like that and we looked at it once and never thought again about making a boat to get us off the island.

On a very clear day I can just make out the mainland. Orbur says he can see it too but I don't think he can because he's not very smart and he still thinks he knows a better way to rebuild the airplane.

It took us a year to make tools out of the twisted metal pieces and disassemble what was left of the plane. We had most of both wings and a big chunk of the fuselage and enough parts of the two engines to make one good one we thought. Orbur started on the engine and when he couldn't figure it out I'd have to stop my design work and do it right.

The engine was fixed first because I had to help so much and we took the one fuel tank that hadn't exploded and ran the engine and it worked. We figured we had enough fuel to make the mainland and maybe fifty miles to the City if our plane wasn't too heavy.

The next year was awful and slow because Orbur wanted to change every design I made and nothing would fit together right and all we had was one engine that wasn't doing us any good without an airplane around it.

And then Captain Sunshine showed up. He was just there one day and he scared us out of our wits and he said he had just come over the sea from the City and we asked him how and he said he'd walked and we knew he was crazy.

And he said he was the sun and the light of everything that was and a whole lot of other names that didn't make much sense either. He also said the island was his but somebody had changed it so it wasn't a nice place to live and I said we already knew that.

He asked us our names and I said we were the Right Brothers and we were Wilville and Orbur and we were making a plane and he laughed and said we were wrong and not right. I didn't understand the joke and I decided that we didn't want him around. Then he asked us if we wanted to get off the island and I said of course and asked him if he wanted to help and get off too and offered to show him my final design that was almost done. He smiled and said that wasn't the way and that we should come with him instead and it would be an easy journey but we had to die first. And I called him crazy and told him that's what we were trying to avoid was being dead. And he smiled again and said everybody had to be dead sometime and they could do it with him or they could do it without him.

Then we told him to go away and he did and I don't know where he spent the night but in the morning we saw him walking on the water up and down on the wild waves without getting wet.

And we grabbed him when he reached the shore and wanted to know how he did that because we could get off the island too and he said that he would teach us but we couldn't learn unless we died first. Then he started talking about the sun again and I thought Orbur looked like he was about to listen so I got us out of there.

He was around a lot after that and kept talking about the sun against the darkness and following the light and dying so we could be alive. And he talked about the City like he'd lived there all his life and was going back soon and he twisted my words all around and wouldn't even look at the plane we were going to fly out in. And he wouldn't teach us to walk on water even though he walked on water every morning and he got on my nerves and Orbur was listening a little bit and saying some strange things I didn't like. Then I had a long talk with Orbur and we hid from the stranger because I knew he was a wizard or worse and a lunatic too and Orbur agreed and we laughed at him and Orbur drew a cartoon of him with a big cape and a CS on his chest like the old hero comics and that's how we named him Captain Sunshine and it's the only clever thing Orbur's done since he stranded us here.

And we agreed we'd never get off the island as long as he was around and so we decided what to do and we found him that night and killed him. He didn't fight at all even though he looked strong but our tools were sharp and it was all over in a minute or two and we buried him in the sand on the other side of the island.

Then we had peace and quiet for about three days and Orbur was too quiet and looked sad and I couldn't get him to work very hard at all.

And then Orbur yelled for me and said he'd seen the Captain walking on the water and he was heading our way and I told him he was crazy but then he was there and I was mad and Orbur looked like he was afraid and glad at the same time.

But all he said to us was that death had made him stronger and he still wanted to take us to the mainland more than ever and I asked him but he wouldn't help us work on our airplane.

I told him to go away and he did and I didn't see him for a long time but I did see him talking with Orbur once but Orbur wouldn't talk to me about it. I was worried that the Captain would change his mind and teach Orbur how to walk on water and Orbur would do it and not tell me and they'd leave me on the island and I was more careful not to leave him alone after that.

Then Orbur was sick for a while and I finished the plane but Orbur didn't want to believe it was done and I was right after all.

Everything was fine but then Captain Sunshine did it just like I knew he would. He came to our cave when it was dark and said he wanted to take us to the City and looked at Orbur and Orbur said yes and I yelled no and Orbur cried and ran to him and he opened his arms and grabbed him and Orbur died.

I ran and didn't look back and hid in the rainy darkness and kept quiet when Orbur called my name but I knew it was only the wind.

Everything was quiet in the morning and I walked around the island and couldn't find anybody and I knew Orbur was dead and thrown into the sea and he was waiting to kill me too.

Then I saw them both and they were on the water walking and they were moving toward the mainland where the City was.

And I stood on the cliff and screamed and called them liars and traitors and everything because they were and he'd lied about walking on the water and Orbur was leaving me like I knew he would because he wasn't smart enough to stay with me.

And I screamed until I lost my voice and they were out of sight and the sea fog came and I was glad I hadn't listened to them and I was still alive.

Tomorrow when the sun comes up I'll fly the plane to the mainland and wave to the water over their graves and laugh when I see the City but it's dark and the wind is howling so loud now and I can't hear the sea any more.

###

HENDERSON'S LION

I first met Henderson when he moved into the abandoned house that stood almost alone out where the savannah met the jungle.

"Why so far out?" I asked him.

"Once the village was bigger," he answered, "and the wilderness did not creep in so far. Look how grand these houses were."

"I know," I said. "They are still grand. I have lived here all my life, and I am too old to move. Why did you not stay in the village, where it is safer? There are too many lions here."

"Every place is a jungle at heart," he said. "Some parts are just worse than others. And besides, the really big ones don't come into the village."

He eyed the long rifle in my arms and the way I scanned the jungle even as we spoke. "I suppose you are a great lion hunter as well," he said - with just the hint of a sneer in his voice. "And eager to show your collection."

"If you wish," I shrugged. "I did not gather their skins that others might see them."

"Then why?"

"They are there to remind me of the peril that is always at hand. Lions roam freely, and no one is ever safe unarmed and alone."

We entered my own house, where Henderson seemed disappointed at the size of most of my furs. "How can a mere cub be a threat to you?" he asked.

"Once grown, it would be a great threat to me - and perhaps to others as well," I replied. "Even as a cub, it threatens the weak and the helpless."

"Some of these furs are tiny," he said scornfully. "It is no sport to slay these."

"It was never a sport to begin with. It is war."

"You must have killed them right in the den."

I nodded. "Before their eyes were even open. It is not possible to be too harsh with lions."

"Mighty hunter - bashing helpless little balls of fur."

"I take the first chance I'm given. I hunt them from the heights, with binoculars and rifles; I hunt them from blinds in the trees; I lay traps for them where they pad. I seek them out - I do not wait for them to come to me. And I have mercy upon none."

"All these little skins on your wall aren't very impressive. I've seen some really big skins elsewhere - and I plan to have the largest ever seen. Perhaps I shall even kill the Prince of Lions."

I shuddered. "No one can kill the Prince of Lions," I said. "It will take a mightier hunter than all of us put together. The lions may rule the grasslands - for now - but let us kill as many as we may. Perhaps the greatest hunter of all shall one day slay the Prince of Lions, and bring their rule to an end."

Then he went his own way, and I saw little of Henderson after that. He made few trips to the village, and he did not gather with the rest of us hunters to talk over the ways of lions, to sight and clean our rifles, and to keep one another wise and wary.

But weeks later, only a few paces from Henderson's house, I did come across a pile of bones - not human, but cut by human hands - and marked with alarm the evidence that one of the great cats had come there often to feed. I judged from the tracks that it had been a young one - young, but large enough to have eaten a man, given the time.

I found Henderson at home. "What lion dares to kill and eat within sight of your house?" I demanded. Then I understood why the bones had been cut and not dismembered. "You are feeding him!" I burst out.

"Of course," he said calmly. "This one is only an ordinary lion, and I want him to be great when I slay him. One day he scratched at my door - just a tiny and playful lion - a hungry cub that couldn't possibly hurt me. But I knew if I waited until he grew up, I would have a *real* lionskin. So I found him milk, and fed him, and watched him scamper back into the underbrush. He came back from time to time, and whimpered at my door - yet he wasn't big enough to shoot, so I fed him instead. Finally he grew big enough to growl instead of whimper, and to eat chickens instead of drinking milk. Then he began to roar instead of growl, to devour great hunks of beef instead of chickens.

"He grows bigger - and more careless - every day. He is all but tame now - I can feed him out of my hand. He prowls boldly here, even in the noonday sun, and when it is time to finish him it will be an easy shot. A grand prize, but an easy target. You too would have great trophies if you tamed and fattened them first."

"You are a fool," I replied. "A *great* fool."

"No - I am a bold hunter, and you are only an old hunter who would shoot his own shadow in fear."

"You are a bold hunter, and perhaps I am only an old hunter. But there are no old, bold hunters."

He smiled again, and said nothing.

"I cannot hunt this lion for you," I continued. "He lies in wait for you alone. It runs from me, and I cannot kill it. Only you can face it. That is one of the rules of the jungle: I cannot hunt your lions, and you cannot hunt mine. I can help you clean your rifle, and I can give you ammunition. I can show you how to track and aim and squeeze the trigger with a steady hand - but I cannot kill your lions for you."

"You do not need to - it is *my* lion. And all who come to see its skin will remember Henderson's Lion."

We parted again, and I did not come his way again until the day I heard roaring and smelled death in the air and tracked it to the clearing behind Henderson's house. There had been no ambush, but a confrontation in the open.

I found his gun first. It had not been fired for ages, and its once-fine barrel had burst in Henderson's moment of need. Then I found his hat, and a bloody trail that led off into the shocked and silent wilderness. Through the tops of the nearby trees I could see the dark birds beginning their spiral descent.

I went into the empty house. There were few pelts to be seen, for he had carefully reserved the whole wall for the one marvelous trophy that had so far eluded him. The wooden plaque on the bare wall read simply "Henderson's Lion." He had left abundant room to mark the day and manner of the kill.

I burned the pitiful scraps of fur and the plaque in the fireplace and left the stones to cool behind me. From his door, I caught a glimpse of a massive mane and tawny shadow moving off into the darkness under the trees.

It would, indeed, have made an impressive skin upon the wall. Unfortunately for Henderson, it was still wrapped around the lion.

The house stands alone and empty again out beyond the village. It will not stay empty for long: someone else will surely move in. I hope whoever comes will be prepared for the lions.

###

CONCRETE AND THE SEA

The change was abrupt. She wondered where she was. There was no freeway - no cars, no horns, no concrete.

Sand. Water. Air. And she stood alone on the quiet beach. Where was her car? And the truck that had so suddenly appeared in front of her? The strident echo of the air horn had quite faded now, replaced by the wordless singing of the wind.

The sea played at her feet, rearranging the sand. She had the sensation of having just emerged from the water. She was not wet, but felt for the first time in her life absolutely and deliciously clean. She stooped and tasted; the ocean was fresh, not salt, and cool with a rare wildness.

She became aware of sound in the silence - sound that shared the stillness without breaking it. Gulls in the near distance. Slow waves shuffling sand on the beach. And music - faint, and far away, beyond the hills that rolled down to the sand. The music surged, and her heart leaped with it. There was joy there, and wonder came to dwell in her heart.

Something large and grandly ponderous surfaced in a vast spray of water out beyond the slow breakers. She was not alarmed; the glimpse of the great dark creature brought her pleasure. It was right; it belonged there - and so did she, now that she thought of it. There was no reason to be afraid - ever again.

She wondered if she would be late for her appointment. *Late*. The word died on her tongue, a strange syllable newly devoid of meaning. She watched the gulls wheeling overhead and realized that time of that sort had no significance - there was only *now* to be considered and enjoyed, and more *now* to come when it was needed.

But what had happened to her car? And where was she? And how could she find her way to ... wherever it was she was going? She could no longer recall. Like unquiet dreams that fade in the light of sunrise, her thoughts slipped away and were gone beyond all recall. She lay on her side and watched the waves sorting the sand on the beach.

The music swelled again from the distance where the hills came down to meet the sea. She rose, and started to brush the sand from her clothes. But her clothes had been lost along the way, somehow, and now she wore a white robe. And the soft wet sand would not cling to it.

Her robe shimmered softly as she reached the line of hills and found them as blue and as purple as her sight had promised. The slopes were deep in heather and rippled with white flowers.

Then she saw that she was not alone. A man in a glorious white robe sat on the beach ahead of her. A fire leapt before him, and the fire sang to the wind and the hills and the man. There was fruit - freshly picked, and even more freshly peeled - and bread cooling on the sand, and a gourd of cool dark liquid that drew her with its fragrance.

A wondrous hunger surprised her. She had never *enjoyed* hunger before - but she had never been this kind of hungry, either. She had no compulsion to eat - it was no longer a need, but purest option and pleasure. Her hunger and this food, her thirst and this drink, had been made each one for the other.

The man rose, and his eyes met hers. She ran to him, laughing, surprised and delighted all at once. And the waves rejoiced along the sand.

###

THE LADY AND THE TIGER

~ one ~

All Alan ever wanted was to see the tigers.

All I ever wanted was to be with Alan.

And all our dreams died that summer.

He was fifteen, and had counted down the days until the circus arrived in our small town and he could see the tigers.

I was fourteen, his little-girl shadow. He wasn't hard to keep up with; on good days he could stagger about on two walking-sticks or canes or crutches, and on bad days he stayed in his wheelchair. I pushed him around then, and was content to take him wherever he needed to go.

The circus was a disappointment. Alan had stared eagerly at the three tigers, but his face had fallen even as he stared.

"They were *live* tigers, but they weren't *real* tigers," he said that night. "They were old, and moth-eaten, and caged, and beaten, and afraid."

The circus moved on, but there were rumors in its wake that a tiger had escaped and been left behind.

Alan had stumped out one night on his crutches to find it. Alone. Without me. Without anyone.

He succeeded, apparently, and all too well. A farmer found his crutches and clothes the next day, at the edge of a field - surrounded by tiger tracks.

Alan was gone.

~ two ~

I grew up anyway, somehow, and came to be years older than Alan had been, and left him behind - except in my dreams. I still thought of him, even while I closed myself away each day in the big office building in the far-away city and filed papers and kept schedules for busy, important people. I remembered him as he had been, and dreamed of what he might have become.

Sometimes I dreamed of tigers. They were always happy dreams, and I was always sad when they evaporated before the harsh reality of daylight.

~ three ~

Something woke me in the night.

It was not a sound, but a feeling - a sense of something wonderful and terrible about to happen. I sat up in bed, pulled my robe tightly about me, and eased the curtain back to peek out the window.

I saw movement below, first beneath the trees and then in the garden.

There was a tiger outside my house.

I forgot how to breathe while I watched the orange and black and white shadows ripple through the darker shadows.

The massive presence flicked across the lawn, and leaped from the ground to the shed roof, and effortlessly from there through the open window.

There was a tiger in my house.

I turned my head, afraid, and watched the black shadow of my open door.

Paws padded down the hallway, and stopped.

There was a tiger in my room.

Its eyes glowed in the gloom. I closed my own eyes, and felt it drifting closer to the bed. Then it was silent, and nothing happened.

I couldn't bear it any longer, and looked. Straight into its eyes. Deep into its eyes.

Don't be afraid, came the message from those incredible golden eyes.

And I wasn't. I forgot how to be afraid.

It shifted its weight, and moved closer yet.

There was a tiger in my bed.

I sank back, and laid my head down, and it brought its massive head down beside mine.

There was a tiger on my pillow.

I watched it, too fascinated to be afraid.

Those eyes. I knew those eyes.

The orange outline blurred, and shrank, and faded into the face of a man.

It was Alan - grown, older, but unmistakably Alan. And Alan was on my pillow.

I forgot to breathe, for a while. But I did remember how to cry.

He slipped his arm around me and waited, patiently, until I was done.

"Is it really you?" I finally stammered.

"It is," he rumbled gently.

"I thought you were dead."

He smiled. "Everyone did."

"But what happened?"

He smiled again. "I found the tiger - or he found me."

"What do you mean?"

"It wasn't a tiger from the circus - it was a real one. A dream tiger."

"A dream tiger? I'm lost, Alan."

"Dream tigers come to any child who yearns for something wild and wonderful beyond this world. This one came to me, and I rode him, and wrestled with him under the stars, and I cried when I thought it was time for him to go.

"But he didn't go. He gave me the chance to join him - to be a dream tiger and fill the dreams of other children. I took the chance."

"And now?"

"And now I make dreams come true. It's my business, and my pleasure. Children dream of me, and I come to them by night and give them what they ache for - a glorious ride on a glorious tiger, a tumble with a tawny terror, a warm and secret memory that won't fade and can't be taken from them."

"But you're Alan again - now."

"When I need to be," he agreed, gazing down at his withered legs, "but not for years and years now. When I'm a tiger, I'm whole - and free."

"I thought you were dead. But I never forgot you," I said.

"I know," Alan said. "I knew your dreams. And sometimes I was in them."

"All I ever wanted was you," I confessed.

"I know that too - that's why I came back for you."

"Would you ... stay, if I asked you to?" I asked.

"Perhaps," he said. "But then I'd always be like this."

I thought my heart had broken before, but it was nothing compared to this new pain. "Then don't stay," I whispered. "Go be a tiger." I turned my face into the pillow as I felt him move away. "But don't forget me, either," I pleaded.

I sensed him melting into tiger once more, and I heard great padded feet on the bare floor. I thought my heart would stop from the pain of him leaving.

Then his weight was on the bed again, and there was something else beside him - beside us. Something soft, and thick, and heavy, like a great plush blanket.

"I came back for you - not to return to what I was, not to join you in this life again, but to offer you the chance to join me." He nosed the tigerskin closer to me.

I stroked the silent fur, unsure, but not afraid.

"Be careful," he warned, wryly and warmly. "I haven't decided whether you put it on or it takes you in."

"Does it matter?" I asked.

"Absolutely not," he returned. "You'll pass from merely dreaming dreams to making dreams come true."

"And if I do?"

"You will be a dream tiger, too, and we will be dream tigers together."

"Forever?"

"It will feel that way. You'll come to think differently about time."

I paused - not hesitating, but only savoring the delicious flavor of the moment.

I didn't think anyone would miss me, really. Someone else would file those papers, and arrange those records, and order days for important people. They would wonder, and maybe they would be afraid when they found all the paw prints but not me; but I was past caring about them as I abandoned my robe and slid my arms and head into the tiger skin.

It was even softer on the inside than it had been on the outside, and I felt it meld with my skin and change it forever. I saw new things with my new eyes, and rippled the strong muscles under my new fur. I stretched languidly in the moonlight, and yawned my great jaws in the fresh delight of a joyous roar.

Alan the dream tiger nuzzled my tiger face. "Shall we go? There are children waiting. They will not sleep forever, and their dreams are fragile and haunted until we fill them."

I nuzzled him back. "Please. It's long past time we were gone."

He led the way through the empty hallway and out the window to the shed roof to the ground, and we both vanished together into the welcoming darkness like striped smoke.

###

someday:

THROUGH THE GLASS DARKLY

FOOLS' FOREST

THE TREASURE OF GALLOWS HOUSE

THROUGH THE GLASS DARKLY

~ one ~

The man with darkness for a face ran to the Station and hid in the gloom when the Train whistled far away in the Wastelands. Other figures, shifty in the shadows, watched with him. The Town, as always, was gravely silent except for a very faint and muffled screaming beneath the earth.

The Station was an open platform with a back wall of dark, unpolished wood. There was something like a fence: the Veil - blue, shimmering, opaque, twenty feet high, running unbroken on the far side of the tracks to the Station and then out into the Wastelands beyond. At the far end of the Station wall was the only opening in all the length of the Veil - the Door. There was glass in the door, and light unendurable shone through it. A sign beside the Door proclaimed *This Way To The City.* And above the sign was a Mirror.

The Train arrived with a wail and disgorged its passengers. Nightshade watched them from his hiding place in the shadows, and saw only two sorts of passengers - just as there had been when he had arrived so long ago. All were disguised and muffled and secret - but there the sameness ended. Most of them scuttled at once from the platform and scurried around behind the Train and vanished into the dark Town standing on this side of the tracks. But sometimes there were a few who were not even aware of the Town - ones who saw the Door and made for it with obvious and delighted haste. But before they reached it they saw the Mirror, and themselves in it. And they were suddenly checked, as though by an invisible watchman. They stood back, laughing loud laughter, and stripped off their disguises and tossed them recklessly into the waiting wooden bins. And as they did so there came that terrible Shining from their unprotected faces and bodies and no one could stand to watch them. But one would hear the opening of the Door and more laughter, and the glow would fade, and the platform would be empty and the Door securely latched again.

The Bar sprawled near the tracks and was the second largest building within the Town. There was never any conversation within its walls - fear and suspicion hung thick in the air and smothered the unspoken words. There was no mirror in the Bar. A solid black painting hung behind the Bartender, absorbing the darkness that seemed to come from everywhere. The inmates of the Town - the Lurkers - slipped furtive glances at the newcomers who had found their way from the most recent Train to the Bar.

One did not have to speak to the Bartender to order. There was only one drink - fiery and bitter and plentiful and free. But the Potion gave nothing save the thirst for more drink and stronger. There was no enjoyment, no taste but the bitterness, no fogging of the mind. But the Potion was free, the Bartender never went home, and it was all there was.

Except to hide in the shadowed cellars and attics or lie in wait for the Trains.

Nightshade watched as the Shiners and the Lurkers sorted themselves out, and waited until the Shining had faded and the Train had gone and the platform was empty. There was no more to be seen, and those who watched did not want to be seen. The watchers slipped away more silently than the wind in the grass, except that there was no wind and no grass. And then only one other was left by the Station with Nightshade.

Only these two were shrouded well enough to risk the light from the Door and brave enough to crawl beneath the Mirror. They reached the bins of the discarded disguises at the same time and glared at each other like watchful hyenas. Hatred boiled between them, and Nightshade's fury proved stronger in the end. The other shadowed shape slunk away from the fight. Nightshade emptied the bins and dragged his treasures away from the rails into the gloom. Choice stuff indeed. A black cloak of darker and thicker stuff than his own, a longer muffler of lightless wool, padded boots great enough to fit over his own,

huge dark glasses - round of frame and free of betraying shine -
and a shapeless sable hat of monstrous brim to shade his
darkened face from all the prying eyes. Hidden within his own
hiding, and shrinking even from the dead twilight spilling from
the open doorway of the Bar, he retreated into the shadows that
swarmed the silent streets.

One could never be too careful. It was dark here, but
sometimes a hideous Shining would flare from the City beyond
the Veil, and one could be caught without enough warning when
the light came. And if the disguises were not thick and tight and
perfectly done, one might even be Seen ...

He well remembered his first High Shining and the wretch
who had been Seen. That one had lost his hat and scarf to a
thief, and was near the Station when the High Shining flashed
and revealed him to all who watched unseen. And he knew that
he was Seen, and all his nurtured secrets known and torn from
him and devoured and lost forever. Empty, he had screamed
over and over without end, poisoning the air, tormenting the
night, until someone dug a pit and threw him down and dropped
tons of dirt after him. But even yet one could hear him
screaming faintly, and Nightshade wondered if the agony of
being Seen ever came to an end.

~ two ~

Nightshade paused, listening, at the mouth of a tunnel that
ran beneath the Gap. The Shining from the Door seared across
the Wastelands in an ever-widening beam, and where it Shone
was the Gap. A labyrinth of tunnels ran beneath the barren
ground.

Only one building stood in the Gap. The Tower. No one
knew who had raised it, or why, or when, or how it stood
without crumbling in the pitiless glare. It was the largest
building, and the tallest, and ancient beyond measure.
Abandoned, forsaken, shunned, unapproachable, it stood silent
and immovable. Light played around its windows - not only the
Shining from the Door but also the painful light from the distant

sky, an echo from the City beyond the Veil. That hateful corona only accentuated the darkness of the Town that hunched shaded by its own shadow.

Nightshade scuttled away into the waiting earth.

~ three ~

Safely hidden, locked away underground behind vaulted doors, he drew his telescope from its secret cupboard and cradled it in his arms. His telescope. If the others learned of it they would seek it out and destroy it. He had once caught a vague glimpse of the edge of his own shrouded reflection in the lens and had nearly smashed it himself. A mirror was a hateful and dangerous device to have; he had crafted his in private silence from bits and pieces smuggled in from the Station bins, from broken crockery stolen from the Bar, all melted down over a tiny forge fueled with the bitter Potion. No one else had anything like it. All other things that had even a remote chance of reflecting or casting an image had long ago been smeared with tar or broken or buried deep in the unquiet earth.

He paced. The bones of old plots littered the floor. To Get Out. To Get In. To escape the Town and its dreadful weight of Lurkers and their ceaseless prying eyes. To make his own place where he could be safe and hidden away. That was all and his goal. And he knew that if he could ever sneak past that Veil he could build his own world there. The Door was too risky, but if he could find the weakest point - tunnel in - he could take the darkness with him. He was a master of shrouding, and knew the secrets of shadows, and perhaps he could even still that awful Shining ...

His plan ticked on to perfect completion. Another hour of quiet digging, a furtive moling of the earth, and his tunnel to the Tower would be finished. He laughed at the sheer ingenuity of his plot. Even the worms in the dank earth wriggled away from the sound.

~ four ~

The digging completed, Nightshade scuttled again to his unholy haunt and scraped the slimy soil from his hands. A covered jar stood stinking in the corner. He took the telescope and carefully dipped the eyepieces one last time in the sludge at the bottom of the jar. Old disguises, stolen, boiled down, essenced, reduced, refined, thickened, skimmed - this was the final midnight elixir to anoint the glass, to filter the unbearable Shining and allow his gaze over the top of the Veil from the dizzy heights of the Tower.

He shuffled through the tunnel and climbed the secret stairs in the recesses of the Tower. The highest chamber received him in silence. Only one window interrupted the stony bleakness of the final wall; it opened out toward the Veil. Perhaps, it was rumored, one could see the City from that window. Nightshade would soon know. He crouched in the shadow at the window's edge and rested the telescope on the stone ledge. He added to his disguise a second and a third pair of dark glasses, well coated with elixir. He placed a shrouded eye to the eyepiece.

The land beyond the Veil dazzled him. The lens coating was just barely enough. There were all the colors of sunlight, and more, and they pained him; things that grew and blossomed, and their life hurt him. But there were trees there - and where there were trees he could plant and nurture shadows.

He could not see the City. It seemed to lie just beyond a range of low mountains. But there was a man in Nightshade's view, and he carried all the marks of one who had chosen the City. Nightshade shuddered.

The Man was standing by a place of still waters, and Nightshade could see the reflection of his face in the water. He was glad it was only an image. He had no desire to see that face fully.

The Man looked up, as though conscious of the eye upon him, and Nightshade ducked away from the eyepiece. There was searing heat and a blast like too-close lightning, and a crackle of flaming light played over the telescope. He dropped it as a hot coal; where it lay he could see that all the black coating had been burned away.

~ five ~

Nightshade stood in his chamber and brooded. There was not enough sludge in the jar to coat the telescope again, and he needed another look beyond the Veil to plot his tunnel there.

Avoiding the eyeless stare of the naked lenses, he hid the telescope and scurried off to gather more fuel for his dark brew.

Time crawled in a stagnation of hours. Nightshade held precious little in his pockets as he approached the Station. The bins there were his last choice. No Trains had come Down for a long time now, but the bins still might hold doubly discarded disguises - thrown away first by the Shiners and rejected again by those like himself. Shabby stuff, indeed, most of it - but he needed it all now for the jar.

He crawled beneath the Mirror.

His name was called. Not Nightshade - not Nightshade but the secret name that no one knew, his private name that he had never ever revealed. He panicked and stood - and found himself before the Mirror.

There were two faces in the Mirror. Only one was his own. The other belonged to the Man from the City. Nightshade's mask burned away in an instant and left him barefaced, hideous, cringing, helpless before the Man and his incandescent face.

Nightshade's first scream woke the town in nightmares, and his second threw chills across the darkness. Another scream - then laughter - rusty and screaling from long ages of disuse and disbelief - and then the true laughter came free and its easy sharpness slashed at the town like a naked sword.

And the Shining came from the platform, echoed by the High Shining from the distant City, and someone opened the Door and closed it again.

In time a few Lurkers drew near, but in the Station they saw only Nightshade's discarded disguise staining the platform. A furtive watcher stole it quietly; piling shadow upon shadow, he crept away into the safer darkness beyond the Bar.

The Town and the Station were starkly silent. The Door was latched again, as always, from the platform side, against the City and the Shining.

###

FOOLS' FOREST

~ one ~

I should not have ventured into the forest. I know that now, but it is too late. I am a prisoner now in this tower, and there is none to rescue me.

"Beware!" they told me. "Beware the Forbidden Forest! It is not a place for any man to enter, nor for maidens like you! Do not pass under the trees - and do not taste the fruit!" But from my house in the shadow of the King's Castle I could see the Forest and smell the oddly delicious fragrance carried on the breeze. The Forest beckoned with cool greenness when summer days oppressed, offered warmth when the winter winds came to chill, and whispered of fresh life when autumn dryness showered dead leaves onto the ground. And whenever I turned to gaze across the stone fence into the Forest, I could see the warning signs posted there by the King:

HERE BEGINS FORBIDDEN FOREST,
REALM OF LOREILL.
WHO TASTES OF THIS FRUIT TASTES DEATH.
DO NOT TRESPASS HERE,
FOR THERE ARE DARKER WOODS BEYOND.
BY COMMAND OF THE KING.

The signs have always been there, from the times past memory when the fence was built. And still the King and the Prince ride to see the boundary and keep it secure, accompanied by the Eagle that perches on their shoulders and hunts with them and for them. I do not understand their caution, for nothing seems to come from the Forest. What do they think they are keeping out of the kingdom? The sights and sounds of the places beyond, and the smells carried on the breezes? But the senses obey no barriers such as this.

Perhaps that is why the fence, in the end, stops no one who wishes to cross.

I still do not know for certain why I chose to plunge into the Forest that morning. I simply went, barely past the signs, not intending to venture out of sight of our own meadows, nor to taste the dangerous fruit, nor to linger there beyond the lengthening of the shadows. The fence was there, just behind me, a long safe pace away. *Other maidens have been lost,* I reassured myself, *but I will be wiser than they.*

But the trees enticed me with their wild strangeness and drew me in, and before long I lost sight of the fence and its reminders, and I abandoned the meadows as well, and I buried my face in those exotic blossoms and inhaled the heady, heavy scent. And the fruit was golden and red and tasted as the fragrance of the blossoms promised, and so I ate my fill of it. After that I wandered through the trackless trees, growing weary at last, and fell asleep on a flat rock warmed by the sun.

But when I woke I was cold and the sun had flown and night covered me. I was crying when I heard the sound of hooves and a man rode into the clearing. I hoped it was the Prince, but I was afraid that it was Loreill.

All my fears were true. He was a tall, shaggy man, and great shaggy wolves trailed at his heels. He cast a shimmer of stars in my face and I fell asleep again.

I awoke again here in the tower of Loreill. Alone.

~ two ~

There is only one window - narrow, with iron bars set fast in the stone. The half-moon shows me nothing but a sparsely-furnished bed, and a pitcher of water on a table under a mirror opposite the window.

I can press my face between the bars just enough to see how the walls drop sheer for many spans, with no foothold. The ivy is weak, and tears away under my fingers, frustrating me with its futility. I dropped a copper coin from my pocket to test the height; many seconds passed before I heard the answering clink of metal on distant stone.

The only exit is the door - old, dark, solid wood, studded and banded with black-wrought iron. It is locked, and does not give in the slightest when I test my weight against it.

It is silent here. There are no birds in the air, no mice in the walls, no crickets under the bed. Only silence. And it is neither the silence of contentment nor the silence of sleep, but the silence of a tomb long dead and forgotten.

The half-moon is setting now. I am afraid to go to sleep, but I am more afraid of the darkness.

~ three ~

I am alone again now, and grateful for it. Loreill has come and gone. The sun shines outside, but not in my heart, and I have no more desire to gaze out the window. I know too well what it would show me - the Forest, wide, green, pathless, inviting - and the King's Castle in the distance. Loreill is cruel, for he has placed me here in full view of all that is now so suddenly dear to me, yet so far away that it might be only a dream shimmering on a horizon that does not firmly exist.

There is no escape from the castle of Loreill.

Not even death.

"One does not die here," he warned me, in his smooth, mesmerizing voice. "My castle is founded on the ruins of First Castle, which itself was built when death was not and fell when it came to be. Yet I have mastered death and made it my servant here, and it takes only those I choose to give to it.

"You cannot escape. If you had the strength to bend those bars and ease your way out the window, your efforts would be in vain; the fall would break you, but not kill you. You would not escape - my faithful Hounds would drag your crippled form back to my feet."

He did not touch me, but he made clear his power over me, and his demands. "I desire your beauty," he said, "and it is already mine, whether you confess it or not. I may conquer your body at my pleasure, and for my pleasure. But I desire most that you *will* it to be mine. That I cannot take, for you must give it freely. Give me your consent, desire my desire, and you shall be mine, and wander unchained through this castle and all the grounds about it. But do this before your beauty fades, before my desire for you wanes, before my interest dwindles, before I cast you into my deepest dungeons and walk away from you forever."

With his words and with his eyes he tore me and turned my soul outside in and left me drowning in my own despair.

"I will come daily, my lovely, to gaze upon you, and to question you of your chosen fate. Do not think that you withhold favor from me - you withhold it only from yourself. I do not need you, though I desire you. There have been many foolish maidens, and there will be many more. I may find one in my Forest whenever I choose to look."

Then he left, and I grieved in my heart to cross the fence again and cling to the stones of the King's Castle.

~ four ~

He comes each day, as he threatened. He seeks my consent with wine and banquet food and fruit of the Forest, with silk and pleasure and music. But I have denied him. Each day he handles me with his eyes and gloats over me, and each day I loathe him more than the last.

Sleep has been my only redoubt. Last night I dreamed of the King and the Prince. I saw them riding forth from the Castle, the two of them gloriously alone on horseback, the Eagle riding proud on the leathered arm of the Prince. And the Prince turned his face to me, and it seemed as though he saw me, and he uttered my name, and began to speak to me, and then something within the tower below shrieked and my dream was torn from me.

~ five ~

The moon grows fuller. Each night as it rises the light pierces the window and falls upon the mirror. I am afraid, for when the moonlight comes I see the fleeting blur of a face in the mirror. I do not know whose face it is. I suspect the work of Loreill, and I despise all that is his, so I turn away from the pale light.

Each day I gaze longingly at the ground far below and wonder if Loreill speaks the truth. Half his words are lies, but I do not know which half. He spoke the truth when he warned that I cannot readily leave; I do not know if he spoke the truth when he warned that I could not die. "For those who are here," he said to me, "this is already death. You cannot die again."

My loathing is such that I will seek the chance of death when the hope of rescue fades. I have not yet given up that hope. I still dream of the King and the Prince. They are always riding, searching, looking, seeking someone or something. I hope they are seeking me, though I am not sure why they should. I have not been a loyal subject, that they should want me returned to their kingdom.

~ six ~

I am very hungry. Loreill brings me food - but it is all worthless fruit from the Forest and stagnant water from the dark streams that wander endlessly and pool aimlessly there. I eat some of it to quell my hunger, but with every bite I despise it more. And the water leaves its own sweetly evil taste in my mouth. It is wretched food, hollow, but I know I will desire more later. It has already corrupted my taste and my needs until it is all that will appease me - yet it will not satisfy me. How could I return to the village even if I were free? I would always yearn for this evil food.

The stench of the fruit is in my nostrils, and I cannot rinse the taste from my mouth. The juice has stained my hands, and my lips have the look of blood about them.

~ seven ~

I tried to kill Loreill today. For many days I have been sharpening the edge of my hair comb against the stone, and at last I tried to stab him. But the metal broke against his chest and he pinned both my wrists in a grip like cold marble and threw me back. Then he mocked me. "Will your force prevail where many magics have failed?" He laughed at my weakness and my helplessness.

He left me then, and I was too numb to even feel despair.

~ eight ~

The moon rose full tonight, and the face appeared again in the window. It was bright and blinding and blurry, and then the face called my name - not the name by which my family knew me, but the name I had given to myself in my secret dreams, the name I ached to be called, the name I had revealed to no one else ever.

The vision cleared - and it was not Loreill, as I had feared, but the Prince! He smiled, and spoke to me again, and then a cloud drew over the moon and when it passed his face and the moonbeam were gone from the glass.

I looked outside, and I saw the moon rising above the tower of the Prince. There was a light in his window. For that brief moment the moon had shone through his window into mine, across Fools' Forest, and he had appeared to me!

He *spoke* to me - he *knows* me - but how can he remember me? And how can he know the name of my dreams? I am only one of his subjects, and we have never met, yet he is indeed seeking me! I resolved to resist Loreill; now I know I have not been abandoned.

The Prince's words still echo warmly in my mind. "Eat no more of this wizard's provender. I will supply you with what you need. Eat it, and it will fill you - but do not spurn the aid that comes to you, no matter how humble the giver. Fleetwing will carry the foul food away, and Loreill will never know that you have not eaten it."

I wondered who Fleetwing was, and how he could aid me. How could food be furnished here, so high in the air? Then I thought of the Eagle, and my heart leapt, for he could take me in his strong claws and bear me away on his powerful wings.

I went to sleep in hope, for the first time in many countless days.

~ nine ~

All that next day I left untouched the food of Loreill, though it tempted me sorely. It was hard to remember that I could not live on it, but only exist, for it holds no nourishment. Had I yielded to my hunger and eaten, I would have come away hollow and still starving; I kept the Prince's words in my mind, and so my hunger was not in vain.

But the night was filled with disappointment. I waited anxiously for the moon, but dark clouds ruled the sky, and I had no glimpse of either moon or Prince. I went to sleep in tears and hunger.

I dreamed of a forest of fruit - all the fruit I could eat, all the nauseous, desirable flavor, all the raging sweetness that enrages me without satisfying, hurts me without healing me, bloats me without filling me.

I sent away the dreams when I woke, but its ghosts are still with me through this day.

I am hungry, and I see no food but that which Loreill sends, but I do not know what else to do while I wait for the Prince.

~ ten ~

The next night was cloudy again, and the sky grew clear only long after the moon had set. But in the stillest hours I heard the soft flutter of wings, and rushed to the window, looking for the great Eagle.

Nothing showed against the sky, though I felt the whisper of feather-fanned wind.

And there was a tiny hummingbird, scarcely the size of my hand, bearing a cluster of berries in its beak. He flitted between the bars and dropped his burden on the window sill - and then vanished, taking my hopes of rescue with him.

I recognized the blood-red berry. It grows out at the edge of the kingdom, on the King's side of the fence, where Fools' Forest begins.

I wonder why the Prince has sent it. I had already tried it - long ago, before I came here - and proved only what others have long said: it is exceedingly bitter, and almost inedible.

Yet I obeyed the memory of his voice, and crushed the bitter berries between my teeth and swallowed the astringent juice and the rough pulp. It was hard, and strong, but it removed the foul fragrance of the fruit from my mouth and the oily taste of the water from my tongue. I felt *clean* for the first time since entering the Forest.

There were only berries to eat, but I was neither hungry nor thirsty when I was done. I fell asleep soon after, and dreamed of the hummingbird. When I awoke it was almost dawn.

All the food that Loreill had brought was gone, and the water jug was empty. I wondered at first if I had taken it in the night, but there was no foul taste in my mouth. I gazed long at the empty plate, and vowed to eat and drink whatever Fleetwing brings me.

But even as I waited for the gifts of the hummingbird, I yet wondered why he could not send the Eagle. Such a great bird would be more comfort than a feathered wisp that could disappear in the palm of my hand. Still I did not despise the hummingbird, for any presence beyond that of Loreill was welcome, and I did not in the depths of my heart believe that the Prince would place an important and glorious Eagle at the service of such a small and undeserving captive in such a forgotten place.

Then I realized, sadly, looking once more at my window, that it is far too narrow for the Eagle's spread wings. Only the hummingbird has room to comfort me.

~ eleven ~

The Prince's food fills me, but it is not sweet to the tongue. I began to yearn for a whiff of the fragrant flowers and trees that surround my cottage and fill the gardens around the King's Castle; the smells here are of old fungus and rotted leaves and dry forgotten dead things.

That night Fleetwing appeared again at my window - not once but twice. First he brought me berries, and the second time he bore me a flowered sprig of orange tree in its beak. There was a note attached to it: *Remember this scent, and do not forget it again.* It was signed by the Prince.

I held it to my face all the rest of the long night, inhaling its wondrous fragrance and all but crying with painful joy over the memories it brought me.

I tucked the sprig and the note away deep inside my dress where I might enjoy them at will, but where Loreill could not find them.

~ twelve ~

The hours of the days crawl past. Each night Fleetwing brings his berries, and each day the taste grows less bitter, less astringent. Somehow the food Loreill brings vanishes; I wonder if he knows what happens to it.

Somehow, the orange sprig retains its sweet essence, though the bright hue of the flowers is fading. I have held and read the note so often I have nearly worn away the writing.

~ thirteen ~

I woke with the Prince's voice echoing in my ears. "Come," he said. "Follow."

And when I sat up I was in a great darkness. There was no light at all. I groped my way to the window, and looked out and up, but even the stars were shrouded by clouds, or else some other darkness had blotted them out.

Then I heard Fleetwing beside me. I hesitated, and reached out for him gently and felt the flutter of his wings over my palm. He dropped an iron key into my hand, and buzzed slowly past me towards the unseen door.

I grasped the key carefully and gratefully and followed Fleetwing's fluttering. I bumped heavily into the wall, and had to grope for the door. I fitted the cumbersome key into the lock and turned it as quietly as possible, and eased the heavy door open. I sensed, and discovered, stairs before my feet; we descended them in darkness, and my heart was always in my mouth, for I saw nothing and felt only the cold stone at my fingertips and beneath my probing toes.

Slowly, so gradually that I could not finger the first moment I heard it, there came the faint clamor of warfare, as great magics fizzled in the distance below and spells thundered and splintered against one another. The sounds grew louder, and we came at last to level ground. I followed Fleetwing along an unseen path for which I had no knowledge or memory, following until my legs grew weary and I begged a chance to stop.

These are waterless places, came the silent voice in my head. *Pass on.*

I walked on as time passed, uncounted and uncountable, until suddenly a faint red glow flared to one side. I turned to it, hungry for the light, but Fleetwing was in my face.

I dodged the hummingbird, and once more faced the dim and distant radiance. I ran, and tripped, and slid helplessly into a pit that blocked my way. There was no way up or out, and I could find no path back. Then I lost sight of the redness as it faded, and sat in the damp darkness and wept.

"Don't leave me, Fleetwing," I cried. "I'm afraid."

After a time my tears dried, and I realized I was not alone; somewhere nearby I heard Fleetwing beating the air. And it was both delight and despair to me, for even though I was not alone, he could not help me out of my plight.

I thought of my orange sprig, and drew it out from its hiding place. Invisible in the dark, its savor had grown faint, and I hoped there would be enough to linger in my senses one last time. I drew it all in with one final breath, and held it there as long as I dared.

And then, even though the sweetness was gone, I tucked the remnant away again. I would not abandon its memory; if I were to die in that pit, I would die with the sprig next to my heart.

~ fourteen ~

The confused noises of the fighting swelled and faded above me, and brought themselves to an end in a rumbling shudder of splintered power that shook the earth and left it shocked and silent. Death and destruction filled the air, and I feared for the Prince.

The darkness persisted, and only the invisible presence of Fleetwing comforted me. I could not number the hours or total the time, but eventually I heard quiet footsteps coming confidently toward me. I made no sound, fearing Loreill. Then the footsteps stopped on the edge of the pit above me, and I heard the Prince call my name.

"Take my hand," he commanded, and I reached up uncertainly as he reached down, and he lifted me up out of the pit.

"My Prince," I whispered, kneeling bruised and exhausted at his feet. "Is it really you?"

A light bloomed painfully bright in the darkness, and when I could open my eyes again I saw the Prince - wounded and bloody, but standing strong and straight.

He glanced down at his battered appearance, and smiled. "He believes he has slain me forever," he said calmly. "Soon I shall prove him wrong. And he would, indeed, have slain any lesser foe."

"Take me with you now," I whispered again. "Don't leave me again."

"I have never left you - it was you who left me, every time." But he smiled, and the warmth in his face took away the worst sting of the words, true though they were.

"I have not finished my work yet," he explained. "I came only to lift you out of this final prison, and then I must go again."

I made a small strangling noise in my throat.

"I must ransom you," he continued, "and not merely rescue you. You have been strong in resisting Loreill, but your taste for the Forest's fruit is so strong and so subtle that, though you deny it now, you would not leave his realm willingly. You would rather die than forego forever the pleasures of that flavor - and die you will unless I rescue you and cause you to hunger after other, higher, older fruits - those that grow in the bright sunshine of my courts and in the fair shadow of my walls. Once they grew here, where we stand, and they shall grow here again."

I tried to speak. "Oh, Prince, I have been ..." I could not finish.

"You have been a fool," he said gently. "But you have never ceased to be *my* fool, and I will return for you. But you must be ready for me, and be ready to act and obey when you hear my voice again."

I nodded dumbly, and he was content with my answer.

"You have been twice a fool, for I sent Fleetwing to guide you, that Loreill might not find you still imprisoned when he fled the scene of our battle. And I rebuke you now, but with soft words, for had you followed Fleetwing in faith, and not turned after the false and deceiving lights, we would have met at the great Fountain before this Castle."

I nodded again. "That pit ..."

"Was my provision for you, that nothing worse befall you."

"Then why was it so dark?" I dared ask him.

He smiled. "If I had left you light, you would have chosen your own way again, and you would have chosen wrongly, and might never have come to the right path again.

"Stay with Fleetwing this time," he commanded. "I leave you with him."

Then the Eagle emerged from the gloom and landed on the Prince's shoulders.

"Yes, my Prince," I said, gazing with awe at the great Eagle but also looking around for Fleetwing. "Where is he?"

"Fleetwing the Far-Seer?" he smiled. "He is indeed a hummingbird. But do not make the mistake of thinking he is *only* a hummingbird."

Then the Eagle swept into the air, and flashed quick circles about my head, and in those circuits at the edge of the flickering dark he was sometimes an Eagle and sometimes a tiny hummingbird again.

The Prince vanished, and his light went with him, and I was alone with the faint, elusive presence of Fleetwing - but whether he was Eagle or hummingbird now I could no longer tell.

"I will follow you," I said meekly into the night. "Please do not go too fast, for I am afraid of the dark and cannot see where I am going."

And I did indeed follow the sound of his wings - sometimes tiny and swift, sometimes slow and ponderous - without heeding anything else that happened, even when a great cry of anger and anguish rumbled the earth and split the everlasting night, and I knew it was Loreill, and I knew it for his death cry.

~ fifteen ~

I walked through the trackless darkness, Fleetwing's flutterings ever before me. Then from ahead came the gleam of a soft pulsing light, reflected from walls of stone, and I stopped in fear of a second deceit. But Fleetwing pressed on, and soon I could see that the light was blooming from a stairway that spiraled down into the earth. We moved downward to meet the light as it grew stronger, and then we turned a final corner and came face-to-face with the Prince, ascending from the depths of the dungeons beneath the Castle of Loreill. He was even bloodier now but triumphant, and the Prince was in the light, and somehow the Prince *was* the light.

"It is finished!" he cried, and Fleetwing gave a great soaring, searing call of joy, and there was nothing else that could be added to his triumph.

Then I looked beyond the Prince, and there was a great multitude of people ascending the stairs behind him. They were silent, but it was not the silence of death - it was the silence of awe, and of wonder too great for mere words.

The Prince gazed down at my surprise and smiled. "What? Did you think I came only for you? I came also for these others - these others who had hope and did not despair even in death, and even these who had lost their former hope in despair. I fought for them beneath the earth, and have prevailed, and now we may leave boldly."

He took my hand, and regarded me kindly.

"If you had been the only captive here," he added, "yet I would have come for you, and paid no lesser price to bring you home ... but you are one among many, if you take comfort from having company in your foolishness ..."

And with Fleetwing vigilant over us we all climbed the twisting stairway and walked together down a long corridor and beneath an archway. We came out into the open, and I looked up and saw the stars again. It was night, but it was only night - a clear night that would soon give way to a bright dawn.

A shining light fell from the Prince's face upon the gathered peoples, and then grew from within them, and at last we found our voices. There were tears of joy, and shouts, and praises, and the Prince was the proper focus of all the good things that were proclaimed.

~ sixteen ~

But our cheers came to an end, and the flaring light around the Prince faded in the growing light of the rising sun. One among us asked simply, "What shall we do now?"

The Prince smiled. "You are free once again, and it is fit that you return to the lands you once knew. This is the path, and straight it leads to the old borders you left behind so long ago.

"But still there is one other choice to make; you must indeed return, but it is not necessary that you each return today."

He waved his arms grandly around him at the wilderness. "You know this as the Forest of Loreill, or Fool's Forest, for so it has been all these ages. And this half-ruined fortress of stone you have called his castle, for so it has been through the countless years. But once this land was mine, without dispute, and this fortress was my palace.

"There is work to be done, for all to be once more as it once was. I do not demand your help, but I do desire it. Who shall give me aid in this mighty work?"

We all stepped forward, not knowing how we should carry out the Prince's will, but only determined that we should do it.

"And you shall help me rebuild this castle. First Castle it was, and First Castle shall it be again."

"With what, my Prince?" I ventured. "There is nothing here now but a ruin."

He gazed at me fondly. "My child, you have seen, but do not understand what you have seen. You have lived all your life in the sight of the stones that once were these walls."

I looked at him, and did not understand his meaning.

"What are the fences made of?" he asked, with easy patience, as if he now had all the time in the world.

"Stones. Many stones, large and small," someone else offered softly.

"And what might have been the source of all those stones?" the Prince countered.

"The old castle?" I ventured, disbelieving even that which I saw could only be true.

"And whose hand made those walls?"

"Loreill? Did he not put them there to keep you out - to protect himself?"

The Prince smiled. "And you believe such a fence could hinder me, riding wherever I wish? We have often ridden through this forest, Fleetwing and I - watching, waiting, biding our time until this very day should arrive.

"No," he continued. "The King and I built those fences, to set limits upon Loreill, and to protect *you* - to keep our own people from the lands Loreill had falsely and foolishly claimed as his own. That claim was suffered for a time by the King, who has waited until now to reassert his dominion."

"And now?"

"And now the barriers shall fall - we need the fence no more, for the reign of Loreill is past, and all the earth is again mine and the King's. Let us redeem this place, and all that lies around it - let us return every rock, every stone, every pebble to its rightful place. All shall be as it was, and better, for never more shall the walls of First Castle be in peril."

~ seventeen ~

"Go," he said to those on one side of him, "return to the kingdom, and to all its boundaries. Wherever you find the old fences, tear them down and bring the stones here to me. If any hinder you, speak my name and bid them aid you. But few *will* hinder you, for they will see the look on your face, and will know that you have been rescued, and will stand aside from your path."

To those on the other side he said, "The forest surrounds you, and has ever been a terror and a dread to you. But the King planted these trees here, a long time ago when the world was young. They have grown wild since that day of darkness, and though some may be trimmed and straightened and made whole again, some cannot be redeemed. Fleetwing shall guide you, and each tree that he marks with his beak you shall bring down.

Bring the wood here to this courtyard, and hew it ready for a great bonfire.

"Do not eat the fruit you find on those trees, but throw it all out into the fallow fields to wither and shrivel beyond all recall. Not even the birds of the air or the mice in their burrows will come to devour it. Yet it will not be a waste, for as it decays and is washed away by the rains its scattered pulp will feed the soil - for it was made of good things once, and good things will come of it in the end." He smiled.

Those he had sent turned to do his bidding, and Fleetwing flew above them. I looked, and all had gone and were busy save me.

"What shall I do?" I asked him, my voice small and lonely in the silence.

He took my hand. "There is a hard work to be done, before the others return. Come, and do it with me, for I covet your company."

He led me to an inner courtyard, where a great fountain lay dry and dusty and filled with the debris of the years, abandoned and forsaken.

"This fountain was once the life and center of my kingdom," the Prince said. "We must clean it, and start its waters flowing once again."

I looked doubtfully at the leaf-strewn basin, not knowing where to start, and wondering how deep one would have to delve beneath the dirt to uncover the old stones again.

"You should simply begin where you stand," he said gently. "When you have done the first part, then the second part will come readily to hand."

So I fashioned a broom from dead branches and twigs, and began to sweep, and I found my strength just equal to the small task.

"They will not return soon, will they, bringing back the stones that were taken?" I asked.

"Soon enough," he answered, "for we are not done here."

I continued sweeping, and wherever I piled the debris the Prince scooped it into his arms and carried it away.

But at last the great stone basin was clear, though it was still dusty and dry.

"How will you restore the waters, if they are so long dead and vanished, and only a memory that none of us recall?" I asked.

"I am the Prince, and I come in the name of the King - even this is not too great a task for me."

"And do you not need rest? I do, and I have not conquered wizards this day."

"I shall not rest until this work is finished - but I know that you are frail, and so we will pause together for a little while."

We sat together on the newly-brushed stone steps leading down to the dry fountainhead. The Prince was still, but ever ready to act, and I was grateful for the rest.

"Who was Loreill?" I finally ventured, wondering if he would give me an answer that perhaps I should have already known.

"He was a keeper of my great magics until he strove in secret to twist them to his own gain. He was banished, and exiled, and allowed to flee to his nest here in the very ruins he had helped to create. And what was worse than his own rebellion, he drew others after him."

"Like me."

"Like you, but not like you alone. You were not the only fool to venture here. There were many others, as you have seen. And there would have been even more, more every year, for year after year without end - but now the wizard is slain and the dank forest is being scoured and redeemed, and the First Castle will rise again to the skies."

He left the warm silence undisturbed for a long time, until I ventured another question.

"Is Loreill truly ... dead?"

"Beyond all recall, and beyond all imaginings - even his own. You shall never hear of him again save in tales that are told of this day, and of the days that came before it."

I was glad in my heart to hear it, but the Prince's voice had betrayed an underlying sadness.

I continued. "He ... Loreill ... spoke often of death, and told me that I was dead and could never die again." I was not sure if I was asking a question, or only telling him something he already knew.

"He seized truths," replied the Prince, "and twisted them, and spoke little enough of the things he could not disguise. Yet in this he was not altogether wrong - you have died, and come to life again, though you are not yet finished with death.

"Death has changed for you, now," he continued. "It can never again bring that harsh and terrible ending. Nor is it as hard and cold as you think it - not now, now that I have been there first."

"I know that I do not understand all your words. Will I hear more of these things later?"

"Once you were mine because you lived in my lands, and because I knew you from afar and on high - but now you are mine because you know me. And now that you are mine in truth and in more than just tradition, you will never stop learning - for there will always be more truths to discover when you are ready to find them."

Then he stood, and we walked together back down into the dusty basin. "This fountain has been dry for too long," he began. "I must wake the waters and set them flowing once more. I shall act now, and you may watch - and take care that you see and understand and remember, for there will be others who will long to hear this story."

He opened the folds of his garment, and touched a wound in his side that was still seeping.

"I did not know you were so wounded, my Prince! Please let me care for them."

"No," he answered, "for they are needful, and you should not regret them. Some wounds are a badge of both honor and love."

He smeared his own life on his hands before reaching down to stroke the silent pipes. "Only this remedy will suffice," he murmured. "The water that once flowed here is the lifeblood of the earth, and only lifeblood will call it back again. It will nourish the land as it did in the beginning, and all the dry places and the brackish pools will disappear and be no more."

Something gurgled beneath the earth, and the ground shuddered quietly, and there came the welcome sound of waters far, far under our feet.

He smiled broadly. "The healing has begun - and never again shall the waters be hindered."

Then I heard the tumult of the returning multitudes, and as we walked to meet them I thanked the Prince for the privilege of standing by his side and having a hand in this work.

"Do not be surprised," he said. "That has always been the place intended for you, and has been offered as your privilege since before the beginning of the world."

The others began arriving with happy burdens of stone and wood, and cast them in sweaty triumph upon the ground. Behind us, water burst from beneath the ground, leaping from the fountain and cascading in the air, with the bright arcs of rainbows overhead. Fleetwing soared above us all, and his piercing cries called down joy on our heads.

"Well done!" proclaimed the Prince, and his praise was all the reward we sought. He turned to us all, and drew from its sheath his sharp and bloody sword. He gazed at it, and at us, and said, "In this dark country I have drawn my sword, and used it for the very purpose of its making.

"Loreill believed that he could slay the one who could not be slain forever - behold! This is that wizard's blood, and is the price of his folly, and is all that is left of him.

"And now I shall see even to that." He knelt at the side of the fountain's fresh pool and cleaned the blade with his fingers and rinsed the recesses of the sheath. We all watched the red streak in the water as it faded and swirled away into nothingness.

He stood again, and held his weapon on high, his power brandished for all to see - the sign of the conqueror gleaming in the sun.

"I have triumphed with this blade," he said. "And now I sheathe it - and shall never need draw it again. Call me no longer the Warrior but the Victor - and now the Prince of Peace."

We all cheered, and he walked among us, and we were content to wait upon his next command.

"Come, all of you - let the waters heal us as well." At his word all the redeemed held hands together and followed the Prince into the pool. It was shockingly cold at first, and stung all our wounds and slices, but quickly grew warm and became a balm to our bruises.

I looked to the Prince, and saw that his wounds were no longer bleeding. But his scars were plain, and it looked as though they would endure forever.

"I have not felt like this since I was a child," I said softly to the Prince.

"Not since you were a child have you been whole, and *clean* again.

"Look at yourself, and at the others."

I looked down, and my tattered, filthy clothes were not merely mended but made new, and all the encrusted dirt was gone. Nor was I alone; all of us wore new cloaks and robes that gleamed in the sun.

And there was more to behold when I looked beyond the clothing. Wrinkles had faded; worn faces brightened once more; bent back straightened; dull eyes brought to sparkle again; lost smiles recovered from hidden places.

"This is your doing," I whispered. "Thank you."

"It is my delight to give you all this gift. I have waited long to see it given - and received, and enjoyed."

"What shall we do for you now?"

"You have all been renewed - but there is still work to be done, and blessings to be bestowed, and old, deep wishes to be granted."

He laid his hand upon one pile of rounded stones, and it fell apart beneath his touch. One of the small white rocks rolled into the waters at my feet. I picked it up, and was struck beyond words to find my secret name written on it.

Speechless, I held it up for the Prince to see. He smiled.

"That is indeed your name, and yours alone," he said tenderly. "I gave it to you before you were born - and it will be our secret.

"You may keep this stone, at the side of the other things you have come to hold dear." And I knew he spoke of the sprig and the note he had written; I pulled them out from under my no-longer-tattered clothes, and my astonishment was renewed when I found the blossoms fresh and the writing as clear and bold as it had been in the beginning.

"How ...?" was all I could utter.

"You will understand these things later," he said. "But for now, let your peace come from trust, and not from knowing."

I nodded, and turned away shyly, and realized that all there held a white stone of their own - and no one else had words to say, yet their eyes said it all.

The Prince led us from the fountainhead to the ruined and fallen lines of rubble that surrounded us.

"Let us now see to these walls," he said.

The Prince laid his hands on the cold and cracked and tilted boulder before him, and it trembled at his touch, as a gravely wounded beast might groan with hope beneath the caress of its master's hand.

"We have come to the end of the beginning," he proclaimed for all to hear, "and now it is time to begin the end!"

I knelt beside him to help lift a stone into place, and we all began our happy labor. First Castle began to rise anew before our eyes.

###

THE TREASURE OF GALLOWS HOUSE

~ one ~

The vast House stood on the heights - enormous, alone, all but empty - and silent behind its walls of stone. There was treasure there, long rumored, but there was also a gallows looming stark against the sky, perched on the edge of a bare cliff overlooking the sea. Everywhere else was green fertile ground, sweeping from the outer walls to the foundation stones of the House and on to the very base of the gallows.

No one could remember when it had not been so. The builders of the House slept under mossy stones in the graveyard, within the shadow of the wall, but their words of challenge endured in the Law - the Law still graven in the face of the great stone set into the hill before the iron gates of the House:

> *He who seeks may find the treasure,*
> *But he who seeks must give full measure.*
> *For he who seeks may end his strife,*
> *Yet he who fails will lose his life.*
>
> *He who seeks has seven days,*
> *Time to trace a treasure's ways.*
> *Time to find his heart's desire,*
> *But he who fails finds doom and fire.*

The Law was simple. Anyone from the village might come to the House and search for the treasure. If the seeker could not name and display the treasure at the end of the seven days allotted, then it was the Keeper's duty to hang him from the gallows and then burn his body on the rock overlooking the sea.

The Keepers lived in the House, tending the grounds, keeping the House ready for those who came to search. The Keepers, alone among the living, knew the secret, and kept it safe from generation to generation. A Keeper without child would come into the village and adopt an orphan, and raise him in the great House with its greater mystery.

Of such a background was Ebeir, the current Keeper and lone inhabitant of the House. On any day one could see the young man at work, trimming trees and stripping weeds from the garden, remortaring stone and polishing the high gleaming windows, awaiting one to dare the gallows and declare the treasure.

In his heart he hoped that no more would come: though Ebeir was young, he had already hanged - and burned - seven men.

~ two ~

The village and the fields beyond it were slowly perishing. A summer drought followed a dry spring, and the worn-out earth cracked when no rain fell. Crops withered in the fields, and herds thirsted vainly in their pastures.

Beyond the village, where the hard soil lost itself in the rocks of the foothills that guarded the mountains, two women struggled together each day to squeeze a living from the dying dirt. Helpless to do anything else, the young Arlea and her mother toiled and watched their land wither.

And when the last of their cattle died, the daughter wound her weary way through the twilight into the village and sought out the elders.

"I am now of age," she told them, "and owe no one account for my words or my deeds. I claim this of you now: summon the Keeper, and take me before him when the sun rises. Our holdings are dead, there is no fit water anywhere, and unendurable famine will soon come to the land. We will die then, for I have nothing, and my mother has less. I will seek the treasure of Gallows House - and if I forfeit my life, I have lost nothing but the agony of a slow death. Within the House lies wealth - and where there is wealth of any true kind there is hope."

Neither words nor tears could dissuade her, and at the first hour of the next dawn she stood with the Keeper and the elders before the graven rock. A small multitude gathered about them, silent and reluctant witnesses to yet another commitment of desperation.

Ebeir stood apart from them all and began, with the hollow voice of someone who does hard and reluctant duty. "Do you, Arlea, seek the Treasure?"

"I do."

"Then hear the clear word of the graven Law. You will have seven full days to seek. On the seventh day, at this same hour, you must stand here again in the presence of us all and name and display what you have found. If you succeed, the House and all that is in it shall be yours forevermore, and my office as Keeper of the Keys shall pass away. But if you fail, then it is my sworn duty to take you to the gallows.

"Whatever you disturb in your search you must restore. You may not dig, and do not need to, for the treasure is not buried. You may not break or destroy, for that which you seek is more ready to hand than that.

"You will seek alone, with no aid from outside these walls. You may not call upon me to help you in your understanding, nor may I speak to you concerning the secrets of the house or give you direction in any way. I may only aid you in doing what you cannot do for yourself. If you desire a ladder, I will bring one. If you require a torch, I will provide one. I will bring you food when you grow faint, and provide you with drink when you thirst. When sleep overcomes you, you will find a bed made ready.

"This search must be your own, as will be your fate, in accordance with the Law that stands written. Is this your commitment?"

"It is." Her voice was faint but clear in the hushed silence.

Ebeir turned to the elders. "Do you so witness?"

"We do," they said sadly.

And to the crowd gathered. "Do you so witness?"

And the villagers replied with a murmur, tinged with both hope and sorrow, "We do." Arlea's mother only cried softly and quietly.

The Keeper looked up at the sun. "The day has begun." He turned to Arlea, and bowed. "The House is open before you. Let us enter, that you may begin as well."

~ three ~

He led her through the narrow gate beside the massive doors, and then turned the key in the lock behind them. They walked slowly across the quiet expanse of the grounds, winding their way through the maze of gardens that beckoned her to linger and enjoy. But she kept her eyes focused on the House as it loomed ever larger before her.

He brought her up the wide stone stairs and into the great main door, swung wide for them and waiting. She stepped into the gloom, and found the House yawning huge and cavernous before her. Struck by its grandeur, she halted in the vast hall and stared at all the splendor that no living soul save Ebeir had ever seen.

Ebeir's voice sounded in her ear. "I may help you look for what you seek, but I am not to help you find it."

She thought about his meaning, and nodded. "I will ask no unseemly questions, then. But I will ask questions, and you may answer them or not."

"And I will answer all that I may."

And true to his word, he stayed beside her all that day in her wanderings, patiently answering her countless queries. "Where does this stair lead? Which direction does this window face? How many levels have we descended? How tall is this tower? What manner of wood is this?" These questions, at least, he could answer for her, and did so gladly.

None of the answers helped her very much. One day quickly vanished - one-seventh of the rest of her life, perhaps - and she still had no clear idea of the extent or plan of the House. House, even, was not a true name - this building was more like a walled city, reaching farther back toward the sea and soaring higher into the sky and delving deeper into the earth than she had realized. It seemed to her now that it had appeared smaller from the outside. She did not imagine that she was the first to gain that knowledge, or the first to swim in the waters of increasing despair.

At the end of the first day, she sank wearily into the soft embrace of the bed made ready for her in an ornate chamber. Overwhelmed, she cried herself to sleep - and even then the stones of the House went on and on before her in her dreams: ever-winding stairs, tall towers, deep cellars that wound down beneath the very roots of the bedrock. There were too many places in this one place, and she was one searcher alone.

Her sole comfort was Ebeir; he, at least, had not deserted her in her confusion and grief, but had given her all the aid and company his station had allowed.

~ four ~

When she woke on the second morning she thought to ask Ebeir for quill and parchment. He provided them readily, and she set to making a plan of the House. Even by sketching roughly and quickly, the afternoon was beginning before she finished.

She looked sadly at Ebeir. "I know you can't tell me where the others have already looked. I'll start at the bottom - the deepest cellars - and search upward from there."

He nodded, agreeing, as always, and accompanied her to the first stairwell, leading her down and away from the open sky.

~ five ~

She awoke suddenly in the chair, her face flat on the map. She was stiff, but not cold, for a fine blanket with the crest of the house had been draped over her shoulders. The candle had long since burned out, and the puddle of dripping wax had cooled in wandering fingers across the table.

A few areas had been crossed off her map with hasty penstrokes, the exhausting but meager accomplishment of the previous day.

Ebeir was nowhere to be seen, but he appeared as soon as she called out for him, in a voice scratchy from the cold and unused in the night. He brought her food, and she gazed at him with tired but grateful eyes. Outside, the night was yielding its rule to the pale light of dawn.

The third morning beckoned, though the first rays of the beautiful sunrise seemed to her to be the searching beacons of doom.

~ six ~

"While there is still day," she said, "I will stand at the high windows and see what I may see upon the roofs. When the light fails, I will continue in the great halls below ..."

She rolled up her sketches and stood. "When I was a child," she said reluctantly, "I heard of a prophecy - not carved in stone, that I know of, but very old and weighty indeed, and not to be disregarded lightly. It says that no man shall ever find the treasure."

"I, too, have heard this saying," he agreed, "though it is not written in my records, and I do not know where it comes from, and cannot vouch for it. I cannot tell if it is wishing or wisdom, or the dark despair of someone who tried - and failed. It is a prophecy that I hope will one day be proven wrong, for it seems only a futile falsehood that holds no hope. Why else would this House be here, and all who dare be invited to find its treasure?"

"Yes, Ebeir, but I am no man."

He nodded, and she knew that their thoughts ran together.

"Has any woman ever sought the treasure?" she continued.

"I know of none," he answered, "and perhaps it is true that a woman may discern what no man has ever discovered. Long into the first night, after you fell asleep, I searched the ancient records. You, I have all reason to believe, are the first.

"May you also be the last, and the one who succeeds."

~ seven ~

And so her days of exploring passed in waves of despair and delight, as she marveled at the wonders around every corner but found no hiding places, no secrets, no revelations.

"I am no closer to my goal than when I began," she said as they walked away from a wing of rooms she had spent hours examining - in vain. "This quest would be unbearable," she continued, "if it were not for your kindnesses. Thank you."

He returned her smile with a sadder one of his own. "I hope it will make a difference in the end. I have offered kindness before, and it was swallowed up in the shadows of failure."

"It is a deep pity that you cannot share all you know. I will most likely give my life for my failure, as all the others have done before me, and all this will remain untouched and unenjoyed and uninhabited - save for you, and the Keepers who come after you."

"It would be folly for me to explain," he responded, "for if I told you the great secret of this House you would not readily believe it. The truth must dawn on you from the inside before you can claim it as your own understanding."

She wondered if his words held double meanings, but she believed him and held her tongue.

~ eight ~

"This is the next-to-last sunrise," he said quietly, "though I know you count as well as I do. Your search must end, for good or ill, by the dawn tomorrow."

On this day, the most important of all, she could not concentrate. She turned her questing eyes toward the library again, but found herself reading in the finely-bound books instead of paging through them for secret maps. She spent too many precious minutes gazing at the sun's glory through rainbowed stained glass, forgetting that she had first turned to the bright-colored window in a search for cryptic clues. She began sounding the marble slabs of the balcony for hollowness, but soon began tracing her fingers across the cold smoothness in awe of their lofty perfection and intricate carvings. And when she stood in sudden remembrance of her task, she quickly succumbed to the call of the restless sea, watching it from the dizzy heights. The unrecoverable moments ticked away, yet she could not fully mourn them.

"You do not seem altogether disappointed," said Ebeir, as the sun spent its last rays upon the balcony where they stood.

"I feel I must have wasted my time - and most likely my life - yet I have enjoyed every moment when I forgot my mission and lost myself in the beauties of this place. I have beheld glorious things that few have ever seen."

He only nodded, smiling. "Most have been stricken by fear and despair by the final sunset."

~ nine ~

She lay on her bed in the middle reaches of the night, and bowed to the knowledge that she had no treasure to hold in her hand. She rose, at last, and stood at the window for unmeasured time, looking out over the surging sea and down into the shadows at the waiting gallows.

At another window, Ebeir gazed down toward the village, watching a lone, frail figure keeping vigil before the gates to the House.

~ ten ~

The villagers assembled in the grey morning, knowing the quest to be finished and over, whether the end be joy or despair. No one spoke as they watched Ebeir and Arlea emerge from the door of the House and come at last to stand together on the jeweled green sward before the graven Law.

She spoke first, softly and clearly, determined that all should hear her. "If the House holds a hidden treasure," she said, "I cannot find it. I discovered neither gold nor silver, nor jewels of any size or kind."

The crowd murmured in distress, and one woman in particular began to cry afresh.

"But there *is* a great treasure," Arlea continued, "and it is not hidden. The Law says that it is a treasure and a fortune - but it does *not* say that it is riches, or gold or silver to be fondled, or jewels to be held in the hollow of the hand ...

"The treasure is this: it is not concealed within the House, nor buried beneath it, nor is it a lost secret within these great walls. The first treasure is the House itself, and in the splendors it offers to those who pause and look for them.

"The gold was in the sunsets that I watched from the balconies. The silver was in the glint of the moon on the wave-tossed waters of the vast ocean below the towers. The jewels are the countless bright panes in the glorious windows that color the light that shines into every room and every hall. More jewels grow in the garden, and brighten the day for the wanderer. And beyond the gardens are long-fallow fields of rich earth, and sturdy granaries ready to receive the bounty.

"This treasure I now name, and I claim that treasure by right of the challenge that was issued on this rock to our ancestors so long ago."

She fell silent, and Ebeir slowly stepped forward, looking neither at Arlea nor at the multitude until long heartbeats of silence had passed.

"You have rightly discerned the treasure," he proclaimed, "and therefore the House is yours." He waited, smiling, until the cheers and screams had died away again, and Arlea had welcomed her mother into her victorious embrace. "I have kept the key for all these years, as did those before me, with much wonder but a heavy heart - against the longed-for day when one would come who would see past the lure of a lowly, perishable hoard of gold and silver and jewels, and embrace this House as beyond all riches and all secrets and all mysteries it might contain.

"Perhaps, in the end, it took a woman's heart to see what has been an open secret for all these ages.

"And now it is my joy to discover that we, all the Keepers through the ages, have kept this key for you - so I surrender it to you, willingly and with a light heart. This House is yours, and I name you its Lady. May you and all your household be blessed."

He brought from a holder at his belt a massive bronze key, and surrendered it with a flourish that had seldom been practiced but needed none.

She took the key and turned it gently and lovingly in her hands. "Is this indeed my house now, to do with as I please?"

"It is."

She was silent for a long moment, gazing up at the vast structure, at the swirls of stone battlements and gleaming windows - and at the stark outlines of the gallows. "Has it always been known as Gallows House?" she finally asked.

"So it has been, past anyone's memory. The records say that it had another name, once, but beyond that is only silence."

"Then let its name no longer be Gallows House, but Harvest House; let us tear down that ancient tower of death and use its wood for nobler purposes, and let us place a stone of honor and memory on the cliff for all who dared - and failed."

Then she turned to the villagers again.

"I have spoken of one treasure, with all its multiplied facets, but in all truth there is a second treasure, a secret of which the legends do not speak: that treasure is Ebeir. He alone knows the ways of this House, inside and outside, in heat and cold, in sunshine and rain ... I would not willingly waste that knowledge.

"It is not meet that I should rule that House alone, or that Ebeir should depart from the House and these grand estates preserved and guarded by his lineage.

"I ask him now, before the people assembled, if he will continue his duties, retaining his post as Keeper of the House, to be its steward with dignity and honor and compassion, that all within its walls may find it a place where joy and justice dwell."

She turned to him. "Ebeir, I have no power to command you; therefore I presume upon both new friendships and old traditions, and ask you to remain, and join me in guiding and protecting all those who come to live here." She stretched out her hands, and heavy upon her open palms was the great key. The crowd watched and held breath with her.

He stood silently, for once cut off from the comfort of ritual and familiar tradition. "I will," he said at last, "and gladly, if that be your wish."

"It is my wish," she responded, "and also the duty I lay upon you, for I will not keep this House for myself alone, or even for my family.

"This whole village suffers, for the ground is poor without the walls, from the poverty of too many harvests. Yet there is fertile ground within those stone walls, and more than plenty of it. Who holds the key to that House holds the wealth of the soil as well.

"All that we have built for ourselves leans, and crumbles, and returns to dust, but this House stands solid and unchanged."

At her command, Ebeir unlocked and swung open the massive and ancient gates; she entered with him in joy and triumph, and beckoned the people to follow them. They came, hesitantly, and stood on the edge of the unimaginable greenness.

"I found seed in the storehouses," she said to the people, "and grain in the granary, but not enough to be reckoned as riches beyond measure. But there is enough that we may till and plant now, and may soon have an unexpected harvest from these rich fields.

She looked to Ebeir again. "Find them each a plot, and dispense some of the seed. Let the old ground without have its rest, and let the fallow fields here be awakened.

"After that," she requested, "find each family a suitable home within the House, for there are many rooms in that mansion. Let there be life and laughter within, and lights, and food prepared and food shared, and an end to the misery of the life that came before this."

She caught his arm gently as he turned to do her bidding. "This House has long had a steward, and still needs one," she said softly, "and perhaps it shall prove that it needs both a Lady and a Lord. Let us do now what is needful, and what comes after that we shall see."

###

elsewhere:

THE FATE OF THE MOOR-WITCH

TEETH IN THE NIGHT

THE WHEEL OF THE SKY

THE FATE OF THE MOOR-WITCH

Love had passed her by, or so she thought; perhaps it was more fair to say that she had chased love away with her fierce demands. Whatever the cause of her lot, it brought her only bitterness, and much poverty, and a withdrawn life lived on the lonely moor just beyond the sight of the village.

There she built her own crooked dwelling, a miserable hut of fallen withered trees and stray twisted branches. She tried to forget the village, and the village tried to forget her. So the years passed, and her worn clothes grew dark with dirt and distrust as she longed and ached for that which she could not have.

"If love will not come to me," she said to herself and the lonely gloom, "I shall draw it to me. And if I cannot draw it, I will curse those who have it and will not give." She smiled a grim smile. "If I cannot have love, I shall at least have power."

From the bottom of the worn bag that held her few possessions, she drew out the one object that had long intrigued and frightened her - an ancient, dusted book, its leather worn by many hands and the passage of unguessable time, its covers marred and mottled with deep and disquieting stains. It was a dark book, with a yet darker past; she shuddered when she thought of how it had come to her.

But now she turned to it, and strove to call forth its magics. In the day, when light brought hope, she mixed love potions; in the night, when shadows shrouded her in despair and all hope was lost again, she cast spells of death and bitterness, betrayal and long-held hatred.

The villagers saw the strange lights and heard the odd sounds and smelled the rank odors on the breezes and felt the tremors in the earth; they both hated and were afraid of the witch who dwelt upon the moor.

But her efforts and their fears were all in vain; not only was she a poor woman, but she was a poorer witch. Yet she did not relent until all had been tried - the light magic and the grey, the grey magic and the black, the black magic and that nameless arcanity that was itself a curse, born in the ever-lightless regions far beyond mere blackness.

And when all her curses and incantations had fallen empty and unanswered upon the stony ground, she turned with trembling hands to the final spell - a dreaded one; those who had uttered it had never been seen again in the land of the living.

"Perhaps they performed it wrongly," she muttered to herself, "or used withered weeds and pale potions. But there are no choices left. I will draw down fire from heaven, or else up from hell - and perish brightly."

Though it would not be swift, and would not be easy, and would come only at great cost, she pressed on with the attempt. Over many days she gathered the oils and ointments, sought the dusts and crystals, and cautiously lined the secret patterns on her floor.

Yet on the morning when all her deadly preparations stood ready, she was interrupted. A cat came to her lonely door - a black cat, tall and lean and hungry and bold.

"Go away!" she cried. "This is no place for you! And besides," she added, "don't you know what I am?"

The cat ignored her complaints, and made a figure eight around her tattered-stockinged legs - then entered the hut. There in the dusty gloom he pounced, as though a flitting mouse had caught his eye, but he only succeeded in marring the careful markings on the floor. He batted the special stones into a new and unmeant configuration, scattered the colored powders that formed the roads of magic, and rattled the crusted dishes until they spilled their foul potions.

Her anger rose hotly; not for many months again would the planets roll to gleam in their proper places, and it would cost her long hours of effort to gather again the obscure elements crucial to the spell.

But her anger slowly dissipated as she felt his silky fur and watched him nuzzle out the few crumbs that had fallen unheeded from the slanted table. And the last shreds of her rage evaporated when she found some soured milk in a jar and poured it into a cracked saucer for him. The cat, uncomplaining of either the fare or the crockery, and unmindful of the chaos he had created, bent his attention to the offering.

Every witch needs a familiar, she thought. *And what better than a black cat?* "I'll name you Scrubb," she said. "Will you stay with me?"

The cat kept his face turned to the scant contents of the saucer, but she could hear his rising purr in answer.

He proved his loyalty in the days and weeks that followed, for he seldom left her side; he was there when the grey dawns broke, keeping her withered body warm; he was there, rubbing her ankles, when she stared in stoniness at the empty skies; he was there when she turned the fraying pages of her book and wondered what spells she might have left undone. The silence no longer oppressed her, for he either inhabited the stillness comfortably or broke it with his plaintive talk and soft rumblings. And the mice that had long nibbled her food and plagued her nights soon vanished, in a display of that quiet magic peculiar to cats.

Yet she despaired of love, and power, and one night she closed her book at last. "All my magics have failed, Scrubb. What can I do?" She stared at her companion, and what was left of her aching heart broke from loneliness. "I wish you could talk," she whispered.

"Oh, but I can," answered the cat.

A thunderous silence followed while Scrubb calmly licked his tail.

"You never told me you could speak!" she finally gasped.

"You never asked me if I could," Scrubb replied, breaking off the conversation to lick his tail again.

There was no reply.

"Well, I *did* speak," continued Scrubb, "and yet you have no words for me. Have you nothing to say? Or does the cat have your tongue?"

"Oh, Scrubb ..."

"Ah, and I have answered to that, even though you named me wrongly," said Scrubb.

"And what is your proper name?" she asked faintly.

"Among other true names, my name is Love. I came in answer to your prayers, but you were looking for other answers, and did not see me for what I am."

She laughed - a rusty sound, with much derision and little joy. "There is no love in this house - I have summoned it here so many times, and all in vain."

"You cannot command love, yet he may deign to be called. And have I not loved you? Have I not eaten the scraps from your table, and never complained? Have I not made this humblest of all houses a place where rats and spiders dare not tread? Have I not kept you warm at night, and purred comfort into your ear? Did I not overlook the kicks and harsh words you aimed at me in anger at yourself?

"Yes, I have loved you much - and you have loved me a little in your turn. It was only a little, but it was enough to keep your heart alive. You fed me scraps from your own plate, and a bit of milk besides, and made room for me on your tattered pillow, and you were sorry after your anger was spent."

She bent her head, and the cat with his sharp eyes could see the hint of a tear, and with his swiveling ears feel a faint tremble in the air. "I had given up hope that love would come to this house," she whispered.

"This is barely a house," he replied softly, "and even less a home. But Love is always at home - and it is not always what you expect, even if it is what you have looked for."

She stared at him long and longingly. "And you, Love - are you really only a little cat?"

"Not at all - although, if you should see me as I am, you would perhaps note some resemblances."

"Can I not see you as you are?"

"Only if you will see yourself as you are - or rather, as you will be. You cannot look upon me and not be changed."

"Will it hurt to be ... *changed* ?"

"Yes, it will," he said, "but it will be a good pain to have endured, and you shall never afterwards wish it were undone."

"All right, then," she said wearily, "please be yourself, and let me be myself."

"You tried to call down fire, and failed. I will call down a different fire, and prevail."

That night the villagers saw lightnings in the sky and strange rolling flames upon the moor. Some claimed to see a whitely radiant lady, clothed only in the glory of her flowing hair and riding bareback on a roaring lion.

A few of the braver sort ventured out on the moor the next day, when all was quiet and there was no sign of further fury. They found only an abandoned hut, and a pile of black vile clothing puddled together as if the owner had ceased wearing them in the span of an instant. Some said the witch had melted at last; others said unearthly fire had consumed her; others said a great beast had taken her, or that she had gone to the far lands over the mountains. Perhaps all these thoughts were more true than they knew.

###

TEETH IN THE NIGHT

Wolves had returned to the valley, and the people were afraid. Every night the howls grew louder and more frequent and closer to the village, and every morning there were new tales of livestock lost in the darkness - cattle, sheep, even guard dogs.

The old farmer living between the huts and the river's bend worried about the wolves. "They will soon eat all that is to be found unprotected near the forest," he said to himself. "Then they will ravage the houses, and the other farms, and then they will come for my sheep. And perhaps in the end they will come for me, too - perhaps even tonight."

He lived alone, and was all but defenseless, but he did what lay to his hand to do; he repaired the sheep pens and strengthened the latches. He laid in firewood for his hearth and bundled straw for firebrands.

And through the following long sleepless nights the burly, bearded man patrolled his sheep pen, armed with only a stout stick, a brave heart, a hip bag full of rocks, a brace of torches - and his long sharp knife at the ready if all else failed.

He prayed to the unseen powers above the stars for help, for aid, for rescue. "Deliver us from wolves," he whispered. "Deliver us from wolves."

For two more long nights and the too-short days in between, he kept his vigil. He lost no sheep, but all his sleep. When the third day dawned at last, the cries of the wolves faded away, and he slept in the warm sun on his doorstep, too tired to return to his straw bed inside.

When he woke, the sun was high overhead, and there was a dog at his feet - a dog so small and ridiculous that he laughed aloud at it. A broad-chested but gaunt animal with a happy, harmless face - a whimsical, short-legged creature with long ears that sometimes stood straight up, but threatened the ground when they drooped.

He laughed again, and beckoned it near. "Welcome, small friend," he said. "I have not seen you before, though I know all the animals in these parts."

The dog flopped down beside him and panted contentedly, receiving a rub behind the ears as though it were only his due.

"Wretched thing," the weary farmer murmured, "I have little, but you are welcome to a share of all I have."

The dog stayed with him that day, sleeping in the sun or following him around as he completed his chores.

But the dog disappeared after their meager supper, and the farmer could not find it anywhere before the shadows began to gather. He cursed it briefly for deserting him when he most needed help, but his anger did not last, for he soon began to worry that it might have moved on in search of richer gleanings - and so would be abroad at wolf-time. And, to be sure, the wandering dog needed protection more than his huddled sheep did.

Dusk fell, and after that he stalked the long night with his firebrand and stick, listening to the howls in the near distance. He was lonely, though he knew he was not alone, for there was ever a vast shadow slinking just beyond the edge of his flickering light. It frightened him deeply, but it came no closer, and was gone before the dawn could reveal its shape to him.

To his surprise, the dog also returned with the daylight, footsore and hardly able to keep his head off the ground. He ate the few scraps that the farmer set out for him, and promptly fell asleep by the hearth.

"You miserable beastie," he said affectionately. "Where have you been all this long night? Hiding from the wolves? I could have at least used your company. But," he continued, "I cannot blame you. A wolf would have you in a heartbeat - and I doubt that I can save my own sheep from attack, much less a small and helpless dog."

He studied the dog, with both humor and warmth in his gaze. "To be sure," he said, mostly to himself, "I have needed a dog - but a fearsome one, a beast fiercer than even the wolves. Instead, I have you. I wonder what good can be found in a hound who sleeps all day and hides all night - but, nevertheless, I shall not turn you out."

That night, the dog disappeared at twilight, and the farmer let him go, and kept his tiresome vigil alone - alone again, except for the dark shadow that followed his own wavering shadow. There was howling again in the distance, but that distance was not nearly so great as he would have liked.

The morning brought him no glimpse of the prowling beast, but what he found was in its way far worse. His blood slowed cold in his veins, for there in front of him on the ground were the footprints of a giant wolf. Three - perhaps four - times the size of the others, with a loping stride greater than his own.

He fearfully followed the tracks on their circuit of his farm, and was astounded to find them changing before his eyes. The massive prints grew smaller and closer together, shifting from a long stealthy stride into a more compact trot.

Reluctant understanding dawning in his mind, he followed the tracks toward his own hut. What had once been the track of a massive wolf had now become the footprints of a diminutive mongrel.

He stopped inside his own home again, and regarded the dog, already dozing by the hearth. He spoke to it, and it opened one eye to return the regard. "You are either a wolf, and I should slay you, or a wolf-bane, and I should honor you. But which?"

The dog did not answer him.

The choice was forced upon the farmer, for that same day his weakness grew into great fatigue, and in his weariness he grew ill; his fever flared as darkness approached.

A wolf howled somewhere outside, but the farmer could do little about it. He leaned against the door-frame and tried, in vain, to summon the strength to go forth and defend his own.

Behind him the dog stirred, and the farmer sensed that what had moments before been a harmless hound was no longer either harmless or hound. Without turning his head, he closed his eyes and levered the door wide for the great bulk to pad through into the unrelieved darkness.

If he is a watcher, he thought wearily, *he needs neither man nor fire to help him. And if he is a slayer, then neither man nor fire will hinder him.*

"If you savage my flocks," he said to whatever it was that stalked the shadows, "then return and kill me as well, for I will have nothing left."

He fell senseless on his rough bed, and the gloom without merged with the gloom within.

All night the wolves raged around his little farm, and all night the howls and snarls drifted in and out of his fevered dreams, tangled with the images of bleating and bleeding sheep. There was a vast shadow among the wolves, and he could not tell whether it opposed the rest or joined them in their destruction.

But the night finally passed, as all nights do. At last he became aware that it was dawn, and he heard the familiar scrabbling at the door.

The farmer roused to let his companion in, and his heart sank as he saw the blood drying upon its muzzle. "You have feasted," he said sadly, "but upon what?" He staggered outside to see what had been left to him.

He quickly accounted for the full measure of his sheep. And soon after that he found the torn carcasses of six wolves, and a bloody churn in the grass where he suspected others had lain wounded before being devoured by their kindred.

He returned to his hut and its sleeping occupant. "Blessed are you among dogs - or whatever you are," he said. "And whatever you are, I still have not seen you clearly. Nor do I wish to.

"What shall I call you?" he asked. "Perhaps I should name you Dudh Leye, the Scourge of the Wolves." He laughed. "No man who sees you now will call you the scourge of anything - but I know better, my little friend.

"Will you stay when there are no more wolves?" he asked. "For surely they will all die by your teeth in the night, or move on."

The dog wagged its tail lazily.

"Then stay, if you please," the farmer said, "for surely there will always be wolves."

He gave thanks, but did not otherwise pray for many days after that, for he did not know if he could bear to behold the answers. The wolves, indeed, soon passed on, but the dog stayed.

The farmer thought, once or twice, that the dog was about to speak - and could have, but changed its mind. Few things, at that point, would have surprised him.

He did venture, at last, to ask a neighbor about the possible origin of the wandering animal. The neighbor, a man with large holdings, only sneered. "That useless beast? He came to us, and we soon drove him away, for he did nothing to earn his keep."

"Tell me," the farmer said, "did you lose anything to the wolves when he was with you?"

"No," the other snorted, "but we lost plenty and enough, before that and afterwards."

"I see," the farmer said - and perhaps this time he really did.

###

THE WHEEL OF THE SKY

~ one ~

The night skies swirled, and some in the village were afraid. Overhead, the silent stars moved slowly, inexorably, forming shapes and wheels and symbols; some who studied the heavens saw the shifting signs and were filled with disquiet, beginning to mutter of strange and dreadful things to come, events that were written in the stars.

And they pointed to omens on the earth as well. "We have seen strange fires on the moor," they said, "and folk disappearing, and wolves appearing and passing away. But *this*," they continued, pointing at the heavens, "will be worst of all - whatever it is. What if it be the end itself, and naught to come after it?"

But some were of a more hopeful mind. "We have had enough of dark and fickle fate," snorted one. "Now is the time for the wheel of the sky to turn in our favor."

Such talk resolved nothing, but eventually reached the farmer's ears. He pondered all these things, and did not know what to think. He gazed at the dog sleeping by the fire, and knew there were many things he did not know. He was content in his world for now, his long loneliness eased or set aside by the presence of the loyal and peculiar hound who had come to him in dark times and stayed.

The nights passed, and the farmer tended to his flocks, and perhaps the dog - Dudh Leye, the Scourge of the Wolves - tended to them all.

~ two ~

Then one quiet evening he was half-asleep before the fire when a soft knocking at the door roused him.

Surprised, he looked to the dog, who normally growled at the distant approach of any visitor. Instead, the dog only regarded him solemnly, without worry.

The farmer rose, and opened the door cautiously, and was astonished to find a striking white-haired woman there, a large black cat perched serenely on her shoulder.

"May we come in?" the cat asked sweetly.

Too surprised to speak, he threw wide the door and beckoned them in.

The cat jumped down and ambled across the hearth. The dog rose slowly and stretched, and the two touched noses warmly but calmly, as though they found pleasure but no surprise in the other's presence.

The farmer could think of little to say. "They know each other?" he asked.

"So it would seem," the woman answered, smiling.

"I should not be surprised at anything."

"No - not if your dog is of the like nature as my cat."

He stared at her for a long moment before remembering his manners. "Please come in," he said belatedly.

She stepped further in, and he closed the door behind her against the night.

She turned her face toward the firelight, and he saw with surprise that she was not old, though every strand of hair that tumbled down from her head was pure and glossy white.

Nor was she young; she showed the weight of her years on her face, though the lines did not detract from her beauty.

"Please sit," suggested the farmer. "These chairs are old and hard, but the fire is warm and bright."

He waved her to the best seat by the hearth, and marked the dignity and wisdom he found in her eyes.

"And who might you be?" he asked, with more than a hint of kindness in his bewilderment. "Are you one like these two, who offer so much more than meets the eye?"

"I am what you see," she answered. "At least I am now. But I *am* one who benefited from the care of an animal who turned out to be more than anyone thought to imagine. As I understand you have." Her eyes turned to the dog, or whatever he really was. "The tale of the Scourge of the Wolves is known to me - at least the story as the cat would tell it."

"Your cat speaks," he repeated, still too stunned to be surprised.

"Yes," she said, smiling again, "but he is hardly *my* cat - it would be better said that I am *his* woman."

"And if *your* dog speaks, then why not *my* cat?"

He could only blink at the woman with hair the color of moonbeams.

"Did he not tell you we were coming?" she asked.

He shook his head, bewildered. "He has not spoken to me."

"Why not?"

Again he had no answer, and so turned to the dog. "Once," the farmer began, "once, I thought, you *were* about to speak."

"You were right," said the dog calmly.

"So you *can* speak," the farmer said faintly.

"I can," came the rumbling answer, "but there was no need. You believed - and you trusted without words from my mouth. Others," he said, glancing at the woman, "were not so ready to give their trust."

"Yes," said the woman. "I had harder lessons."

The farmer had no idea what to say next, and so wisely said nothing.

"This cat is called Scrubb," said the woman into the silence.

"And he is called the Hound of Heaven," Scrubb said simply.

"I am sorry," the farmer offered to the dog. "I would not have called you Dudh Leye if I had known your true name."

"It matters not," replied the hound. "My true name would be a burden on your tongue - and Hound of Heaven is only one of the many things I am called. So, indeed, 'Scourge of the Wolves' is no dishonor, and I will answer to it."

Then the dog turned to the cat again, and they began speaking in a soft language neither human understood.

The farmer studied the two animals. "They are of a kind, are they not?"

"Whatever they are," she agreed.

The farmer and his visitor sat before the crackling flames.

"Who are you?" he asked again. "And why have you and your ... companion ... come to this humble house?"

"Who am I? I do know you from of old," she began, "but you will no longer recognize me.

"I lived here, if you can call it living, for I spent all the moments of my existence striving for the things I could not have. I nearly died here, as well, for the same reasons, and did end my life here as I once would have called it." And she told him the tale of her attempted sorceries so wonderfully ruined by the wandering feline.

"And I rode him - or he carried me - away from here and up the steep cliffs to the Land Over the Mountains. And there ..." Words failed her, and tears filled her eyes.

He wondered what sights had rendered her speechless, but he did not press her for details. Instead, he told her the story of the inoffensive comical hound who had come, he thought, to be protected, but had instead become the protector of his house and all his animals.

"Hear them now," he suggested. "They spend their nights in peace, because of what *he* has done."

She listened. "I hear nothing from your flocks."

"That is because they fear nothing now, and are content."

She regarded the dog quietly. "Have you seen the Scourge?" she asked. "Or only your hound?"

"No. Only this beast, lost or hungry or sleepy." Dudh Leye's eyes were closed as he lay unmoving now in the straw. It was hard to tell if he was listening or not.

"I have seen his shadow, and his footprints," he continued, "but I have no desire to see his true form. Not yet, though I have long wondered if there will come a time for that, for I have often doubted that his story here is ended."

"Those are fair doubts," the woman said. "I thought my life was over when Scrubb bore me away - and so it was. But there is yet work to be done, and little time to succeed, and so I have been ... *brought* back to this place. Peril approaches, and it falls to us to raise an alarm and lead to safety anyone who will listen."

"Why us?"

The cat answered him. "You have seen the disturbance in the stars. You have heard the rumors and the guesses, and the fantasies and the fears ..."

"They are not fantasies," the woman continued in her small, sweet voice, "though they are indeed old fears. What will come is a comet - a god's hammer from the heavens, a vast stone to smite the earth ...

"It will come to pass - but it will not pass. It will strike with celestial fury, and it will smash this place into flaming dust and lifeless ashes. The only way to escape is to flee - and the only safety lies Over the Mountains."

"How do you know these things? Has your journey over the mountains taught you wisdom?"

"I have been taught, indeed, and have been shown. But I am not wise - I only bring you another's wisdom."

Beyond that she would not answer him.

Then he was ashamed of his lack of hospitality, and found them all food and drink.

And afterwards, he asked, "What, then, should we do? Where should we begin?"

"First, we should sleep. Night is full upon us, and the path over the mountains was long and steep."

He knew his own weariness, and sensed hers. "You may stay here, if you wish," he said, "though this hut can scarcely be better than whatever you had."

"It is a needful thing," she answered. "My hut is but a cold ruin and desolation now, and I would not wish to linger there even if the walls were still standing."

"There is good straw, and a spare blanket, and I can gather fresh rushes from the riverbank."

She smiled. "I have slept on worse, and have offered poorer hospitality than this." She looked at the animals. "Scrubb should be at peace in any warm corner - or curled up with me."

He gave his poor bed over to the woman, and spread fresh straw along the wall for the dog and the cat, who seemed to be content - for now - with their own company.

~ three ~

In the early morning she helped him tend to his flock. Dudh Leye and Scrubb had vanished, but neither woman nor farmer could find worry for them in their hearts.

"Tell me more of the Land Over the Mountains," he asked.

"You are not yet persuaded? Then I do not blame you, and mark your wisdom instead, for one who believes only the word of a stranger is more than half a fool."

And she told him all that she could fit into mere language - how all things she had hoped for and longed for and dreamed and dared to imagine had all been laid before her Over There.

"And you will meet the King ... you will have to meet the King, and it will be your delight to meet the king, and you will understand him. He is the King to whom all other kings would give their crowns, the King of kings who *should* reign, everywhere and in all lands for all time ..."

"And he has sent you? To me?"

"Yes, and to all who live here. It was not his command, but it was his wish, and a wish I could never bear to refuse."

"Why me?" asked the farmer, echoing his question from the day before. "Why us?"

"It would seem that we alone have had the ears to hear what was said to us - or in your case, what was *not* said," she added.

"These two came to our valley from the Land Over the Mountains - so do not be amazed that they reason, and speak, and act, for all things are much different there - things not so much beyond our imagination, as simply too *good* and too *right* to be readily believed by simple folk like us.

"That Land endures forever, but this valley will not. Who will tell all those who live here? It falls to us now - to us four. And it seems that those two have already begun their work - whatever it is. We have seen that they keep their own counsel well.

"And ours will not be an easy task. This is a town hard of head and harder of heart," she said. "Wolves were sent to chasten it, and the wolves were driven away to hearten it, and yet no one saw the truth - no one but you."

He shook his head. "I saw little enough."

"You saw enough to believe, and to trust what you did not fully understand. You have been protected here, but even that protection will come to an end. The Hound will leave, whether you go with him or not, and Scrubb and I will go as well, whether or not we draw anyone with us."

He looked toward that hard-hearted village, not relishing the task she had laid before him.

She followed his gaze. "I know your fears - they would have been mine, once."

He waved his arms helplessly in the direction of the village. "Who would I tell? And what would I speak of? A talking cat? A shape-shifting dog? A witch returned from the dead? A stone hammer falling from the sky? I would be shunned as a fool, or burned as a madman."

"Yes - but I would fare no better. We shall not speak of things too hard to believe, but of things the village is all too ready to believe.

"Lay your fears aside, for now, for when it grows dark tonight I will offer you a final proof."

And after their meagre but welcome supper she said to him, "Come with me." She led the way out into the stillness of the night and pointed upward into the starry void.

"What do you see there?" she asked the farmer. "There, in the empty space between the Plough and the Sword."

He looked long before answering. "Nothing moves there, for over *here* do the stars swirl. *There* is only the motionless silence of the mysteries."

"Before dawn the comet will open its bright eye there, and you shall see it with your own eyes. If you need that to believe, then it shall awaken your belief - or else it will strengthen what faith you have already placed in our words."

They went back inside, and to bed, but they both wakened early and returned to watch the sky.

"There it is," the farmer said. He pointed, and they both marked the first pinpoint of angry red light that flared suddenly and blinked briefly at them before the darkness was washed out by the coming dawn.

"Let us go into the village when the sun rises," said the woman. "We will speak of the comet to come, though few will believe until their own eyes confirm our warnings. If our voices are to be heard, we must first tell the villagers of the comet - *before* it is seen, and not after."

"Shall we take Scrubb? And Dudh Leye?"

She suppressed a wry smile. "The people are hardly ready for *us*. But if words from those two are needful, I have no doubt they will speak beside us."

~ four ~

Morning came in all its fullness. The two animals departed silently together, bent on errands of their own. The two humans walked the short distance into the village and began telling their tale to those who had gathered by the well.

"You have seen the signs," the white-haired woman said. "We know them, and we know that something will indeed come, and we know that what will come is a comet. A ball of iron and fire from the heavens ...

"... and all things here will be burned. The only escape is to flee to the Land Over the Mountains."

Someone behind them jeered. "But there is no Land Over the Mountains. That is only a fable, and perhaps a wish."

She smiled. "So I thought, once, but I have been there. It is not a fable, though it may be a wish born of memory and overfilled with abundance. And I will return there, though none of you go with me."

"Is that why you have come?" he asked.

"Yes," she answered. "In a few days, this valley will be no more. I must persuade you to come back with us, and then we must persuade others to come as well."

"And what say *you*, farmer?" a neighbor asked.

"I have not seen the wonders she has seen, and cannot speak of them. Nor have I journeyed Over the Mountain. But I have seen strange things I could never have imagined, and all these things have the ring of truth. I will go with her."

"You are too ready to believe, old man."

"Then test our words at nightfall," he answered. He pointed to the sky. "Tonight, when it grows dark, look to the heavens between the Plough and the Sword."

"There is nothing there," came the flat reply.

"There will be soon - a new sign to seal what you have seen elsewhere in the stars - and when the sun has passed you will see it for yourselves."

"Then save your words for tonight," spat a woman at the edge of the crowd. "We have work to do - return here at sundown, if you dare, and put your promises to trial. But be warned that we have little patience for liars and fools."

~ five ~

The rest of the day passed slowly, and they turned together to the chores of the farm to still their anxiety. "I wonder what Scrubb and Dudh Leye have been doing?" the woman asked.

"I have not seen them since they woke by the fire this morning, but I doubt that they have been idle. They will tell us of their tasks when they are ready. They may be animals, but they are far more than mere animals, and very far indeed from being tame."

"The sun is waning," he said at last. "Shall we return and stand with the people as the stars come out?"

"No," she said. "They will see, and they will come to us."

And they did. Not long after dusk had given way to darkness, they heard the murmur of voices outside.

The farmer opened the door, and they beheld a crowd with both animated faces, both worried and defiant.

"So you have seen the secrets of the sky," he called out as he and the woman stepped outside. "What say you now of the comet?"

A babble of uplifted voices greeted them.

"Perhaps there is a comet," someone called out, grudgingly. "But it will not strike us, for this is such a very small place, and any gods who hurl the stars at us must have excellent aim indeed."

"It will smite this valley," the woman replied, "and no-one and nothing will endure it."

"You are a good guesser - or a witch."

"I *was* a witch" she said serenely. "But that was before I went Over the Mountains. This has nothing to do with witchcraft."

"Then we will not be here when it comes," said a few, already making plans to load their scant but precious possessions on their wagons. "We will go to higher ground across the river. Or even to the Far Plains."

"No ground here is high enough, or safe," said the white-haired woman. "You will not reach the Far Plains in time, and the distance you do travel will not be far enough. The only place of safety is the Land Over the Mountains."

"There is no Land Over the Mountains," someone insisted. "It is only a fable, a legend, an old wives' tale."

"Tales told by the old are not told idly, and even the strangest of legends began with solid truths. Besides, I have been there, and have seen with my own eyes ..."

"So tell us what you saw," challenged someone.

"There are no words for it," she answered sadly. "The words we have are too weak, and the right ones have not yet been fashioned.

"The Land Over the Mountains is not far away," she continued, "though the way is neither obvious nor easy. The path to the Far Plains is indeed plain and pleasant, but it is long, and will not deliver you to safety."

A villager stared at her, incredulous. "There is no path up those mountains," he scoffed, "and nothing on the other side even if there were."

"I have passed that way," she replied softly, "and found the fair land on the far side."

"And you came back?"

"Only for you - for all who would listen."

Another said, "That way, if it exists, is hardly a path - and we cannot take our wagons with us."

"No. But you will not need them. There are no goods or treasure here that you cannot find in abundance Over The Mountain."

The man turned away, shaking his head, and many left with him.

"We have survived many hardships here," one of the remaining men grumbled, "and this comet is no different." Disbelief reigned in the man's eyes, and he turned away - as did, finally, all the rest.

In the end, the farmer and the white-haired woman were left alone again before his hut.

"They are not convinced," she said sadly. "I hoped the visions of the night might do what my tales could not."

"They cannot doubt our first prophecy," returned the farmer. "Perhaps they will let that knowledge grow in their hearts before the second prophecy comes true."

"They have little time - for the comet comes, and it comes swiftly."

"Your words were right."

"Do they frighten you?"

He turned to stare at her, and then gazed after the departed villagers. "I cannot decide if they frighten me or bring comfort."

They closed the door against the empty darkness, and found that Scrubb and Dudh Leye had slipped into the hut and were stretched wearily before the fire.

"Should we ask what you two have been doing?" inquired the farmer.

"You may certainly ask," Scrubb replied. Then he went to sleep.

~ six ~

The next morning some of the fisherfolk were gathered at the river, gesturing - pointing at a large school of fish flapping and jumping and moving swiftly down the long ribbon toward the unseen sea.

The farmer and the woman and the two animals watched from the distance.

"Even the fish are fleeing," said the farmer.

"They cannot climb," replied the dog, "and we cannot carry them, so they must take a longer road."

"So this is the work you have been doing," the farmer said. "I hesitate to ask," he continued, "but do even the fish have names?"

"Yes," said the dog, "but I doubt that you could pronounce them."

"Are you calling the animals," the woman asked, "as we are trying to call the people?"

"Yes," said Dudh Leye, "but we have our obstacles as well."

"Your sheep have not heeded *me*," said the cat. "But there are other beasts they will heed - and obey - if it comes to that." The farmer thought both the cat and the dog might be smiling.

~ seven ~

Another night, and another, and the comet grew closer and loomed larger in the sky.

The farmer and the woman returned to the village again and again with their message.

"The wheel of the sky is indeed turning, but it is not blind fate, for there is One who turns that wheel with giant hands and orders its motions. Yet you who watch are not altogether wrong, for you have read rightly the signs in the stars. Judgement is coming, and surely, and swiftly, but there is deliverance offered even as the comet's shadow darkens the earth."

Yet time and again they were turned away, first with silence and then with curses and finally with stones.

~ eight ~

The fourth night held little darkness, for the blazing comet spanned half the arc of the sky - a blinding, mesmerizing fury.

"We must leave tomorrow," said the woman, "with all who will follow us, be they many or few."

"We are ready," said Scrubb. "Our work is done - and those we have called have already fled, or await only a word from us."

And at the time of dawn they all went one last time to the village.

On every hand the people stood transfixed, gazing upwards at the boiling turmoil of the sky, all frozen with fear and heedless of the man and the woman and the two animals who ventured among them. The farmer spoke to some of them, but there was no answer.

"We are too late," he said.

"They are lost," commented the woman. "I was warned of this, and was afraid that I would see this with my own eyes."

"They stand rooted to the ground, for they are rooted to this ground, and can conceive of no other refuge."

"Perhaps not all have given up hope," said the woman. "Let us go inside."

After the first house he knew why they had returned a final time. Three men and two women were standing outside, their eyes fixed immovably on the heavens. But inside they found a small child crawling, and an infant in a wooden cradle.

Without speaking, they each gathered up a child.

"They will not be cared for if we leave, for only death will take them," she said flatly.

Outside again, they came upon a flock of children huddled in the lee of a stable.

"We are afraid," one of the young ones said to her.

"Then come with me," she answered. "I am afraid, too, but only while I am *here* - and I know a place where we will no longer be afraid."

She beckoned to them, and they followed her, gazing curiously and fearfully at the silent, staring men and women.

In the next house they found an old woman, blind and frail and almost deaf, who clutched at the farmer's arm and would not let him go.

"We shall take you with us," he promised. "But we will need more help."

He looked at Dudh Leye, and asked a question with his eyes, and the cat and the dog turned silently away and disappeared into the fields.

The burly farmer and the woman with the snowy hair worked their way through the silent village, gathering the last few who could be lifted or persuaded. They stood still, and opened their arms to the children who crowded around them, and their hearts were both saddened and filled

"Have you noticed?" the woman asked. "We have all the young, the helpless, the weary ... we have those who have not yet put down roots into this world, and those whose root has withered for lack of nourishment, while those who are solidly planted will cling fast where they are, and will remain, and will surely perish.

"But can we carry all these too small to walk? Can we lead all these too frail to find the way without help?"

He looked at her. "If we must, then we will."

"Some come from fear," she murmured. "A few from love. Others from curiosity. And some because they have nothing to lose."

"But they are coming," he murmured back.

"Yes, they are coming. And I shall be content with that. They will learn more on the journey.

"It is not a place one may enter unwittingly. One who comes for wrong reasons will find a misleading road, and be lost in the wilderness; one who comes with faint hopes and a fainter heart will turn away in the last stages of the ascent, for the final steps are dark and hard. Only the very tiny can be carried, though there is help enough for the old and weary."

She looked beyond his shoulder, and smiled. "And now it is better than you can possibly imagine." She gestured down the riverbank, into the near distance. "We are not alone in our efforts," she answered. "Behold our friends."

Animals of all kinds were crowding up the riverbank - a wondrous assortment of sheep and bears and cattle and lions and badgers and tigers, all moving peacefully but urgently toward the village.

And Scrubb and Dudh Leye were at their head.

"I see they have heeded you," called the farmer. "So many ... and wild beasts among them!"

"Are they not worthy of rescue as well?" asked Scrubb. "And be assured that they will discover what they were meant to be, and they will be well, and all will be well."

The farmer eyed the restless pride. "Do these beasts speak, too?" he inquired of Dudh Leye.

"Not yet," answered the dog.

The woman gestured to the small crowd at her back. "We need your help. We have run out of arms."

"And so we brought many backs, to aid you."

They all bent their labors toward matching the waiting children and old men and women with willing mounts.

The woman turned at one point to find a tigress carrying off a baby in her mouth. She started to protest, but a look from Scrubb stopped her.

"She is a mother," Scrubb said. "She knows more of these things than you do."

At last all were mounted or held or otherwise ready.

"Let us leave," Dudh Leye urged.

"We have no time left," added the woman. "We have done all that we could do, and the end of our task here is at hand. Now we must finish the journey."

Scrubb led them all through the village and out across the fields and toward the first outspurs of the mountains. The man and woman followed behind, and Dudh Leye paced with them while watching for stragglers.

"This is the way?" asked the farmer. "There is no passage up the mountain here!"

"There is, but it is neither easy to find or easy to travel," answered the woman. "Nevertheless, it is the only path to safety." She gazed at the quietly restless lines ahead of them. "And we will take all these with us. They may seem like a burden on the way, but they are a precious burden."

"You each wanted love, and children to share it with," the dog said. "And now you have many children, and many loves."

~ nine ~

They passed over the hills and climbed up and over the long lines of ridges, aware all the time that the sky behind them was growing brighter and hotter. The time for night came, and passed, but no darkness fell.

Afraid to stop, they pressed on, helping and encouraging one another in their weariness; they came at last to a wide ledge high up into the mountains, and Scrubb and the Hound halted them there.

"Good beasts," the farmer said gratefully, "I am in need of a rest, and I doubt that I am alone."

The woman gestured behind them. "This is the last resting before the top - and this time there is something you should see."

They turned and looked out over the valley and the long ranges of rock they had already climbed.

The comet filled the whole sky for one last terrible moment, and then fell beneath their sight. Fire and smoke leapt up in the distance, and the ground trembled under their feet. Immense echoes of the distant impact rolled over them. They gazed at the flames for a long moment, and turned away, and did not care to look again.

"Was it the end of the world?" the farmer asked.

"It was the end of *their* world," she answered simply.

He did not ask her anything again, and had little breath for anything but the climbing. But at last the head of the mountain was beneath their feet, and the sun rose in front of them and the sight before them of the Land Over the Mountains drove the former thoughts out of their minds forever.

###

epilogue:

A CHILD OF THE SNOWS

THE INN AT THE END OF THE WORLD

A CHILD OF THE SNOWS

There is heard a hymn when the panes are dim,
And never before or again,
When the nights are strong with a darkness long,
And the dark is alive with rain.

Never we know but in sleet and in snow,
The place where the great fires are,
That the midst of the earth is a raging mirth,
And the heart of the earth a star.

And at night we win to the ancient inn
Where the child in the frost is furled,
We follow the feet where all souls meet
At the inn at the end of the world.

The gods lie dead where the leaves lie red,
For the flame of the sun is flown,
The gods lie cold where the leaves lie gold,
And a Child comes forth alone.

Gilbert Keith Chesterton
(1874 - 1936)

###

THE INN AT THE END OF THE WORLD

~ one ~

The darkness was alive with rain and the two travelers were lost. On sodden horses, they rode with the wretched air of men who have abandoned hope of food, warmth, and shelter. The younger man, Elan, cursed the downpour and drove his mount onward through the tangled underbrush.

"Do not raise your anger against the elements," his companion said. "It is folly - and our peril could be worse. This might be sleet, or snow."

"You pay no attention, old man. What was rain is now sleet and will soon be snow."

After that they stumbled on without speaking. The sleet gave way to mounting drifts.

How easy to lie down and give up, thought Elan. *But then I would die.*

How easy to lie down and give up, thought the older man. *But even then I wouldn't die.*

How easy to despair, thought Elan. *We do not know if our path is in vain. And if we do not find the Inn ... then my life is only a fleeting banquet and too soon the feast will end.*

How easy to despair, thought the older man. *There is no Inn here, though stranger legends have proved true. And if there is no other hope than this, and this be false ... then my life is still the prison from which there is no escape.*

The wind shifted and roused him. He guarded his eyes against the wet stinging lash of the snow and peered into the darkness. A light twinkled in the distance - and then winked out before he could confirm his vision. *Eyes, I do not trust you. You have deceived me too often before. Still, a great fire smolders somewhere. I feel it - but how far away? We have need of it. And is that the wind, or the sound of singing?*

Elan slumped dangerously sideways in the saddle, gazing through half-shut, snow-crusted eyes at something a long way gone, mumbling softly and with little awareness. Images of another day played in his mind - an afternoon a few months gone, a warm afternoon and a weary rest in the midst of an untraveled forest ...

The brush rustled and the attacker was upon him. Elan landed heavily on his back. The other man's foot was upon his chest and a cold sweat chilled his throat. "Draw your sword - kill or be killed!" Then the man stepped back, and Elan could see him clearly - an old man, but lively and strong, with many scars on his wrists and body, a livid, puckered slash low across his throat, and a roughly-trimmed beard and mustache and long white hair like a waterfall of snow. "Slay or be slain!" the old man cried, and Elan drew his sword. The old man's eyes glittered like twin sapphires polished by the passage of years. A feint, a parry, a slash, and then the old man cast aside his own weapon with a laugh as Elan pierced him through the heart. Elan wrenched the blade free and they both stared at the blood on the steel. The old man did not move, nor did he bleed for more than a heartbeat. His wound healed over like a crimson flower pulling in its petals, and the red smear evaporated quickly from Elan's blade. The old man fingered his chest sadly, sighed, and regained his sword and sheathed it. "My son," he said, "I am satisfied. Be at peace, for I will not draw against you again. Indeed, I will draw for you in your time of need., for you tried - even in vain - to come to my aid. I am Alabaster, and I am cursed, but I am a loyal man."

Alabaster grabbed for his companion's reins and urged both weary horses toward the remembered, elusive sparkle.

"We should go together," Alabaster said. *"Your quest is plain upon your face. You seek life. It is written in the longing of your eyes and the fierceness of your defense."*

"Who are you? What do you seek?"

"I seek that which you flee - I seek the grip of Death, as you desire the embrace of Life."

"I have sought the Fountain of Youth."

"And I the Basilisk."

"The Tree of Life."

"The Gorgon."

"The Golden Apples of the Sun."

"The Poison Well."

"The Philosopher's Stone."

"The Oracle of Oblivion."

"I have sacrificed upon the altars of all the gods."

"Then you have merely followed in my footsteps."

They were silent.

"Is there nothing left, then?" asked Elan.

"There is one last refuge of hope. You know of it, else you would not journey through this forsaken forest."

Silence answered him.

"Beyond this wood, if it lies anywhere, lies the High Country, and at its farthest reach is the End of the World. Some say there is an Inn there where all dreams may be fulfilled - for a price. You travel there."

Elan nodded.

"Then let us go together," Alabaster concluded, *"for we are both desperate men."*

The horses stopped suddenly. Elan, sliding, falling, landed in his companion's arms and was turned to face the ancient stone inn looming large in the darkness.

A child stood before them, waiting, holding a lantern high in the air.

~ two ~

The two travelers slumped before the hearth and let the radiance of the fire seep into their bones. Their raw throats soothed by hot drink, they huddled in thick blankets and waited for the dangerous numbness to pass.

Behind them, somewhere in the kitchen depths, the child stoked other fires and steeped a great kettle of stew. He brought them steaming bowls and more mugs and vanished to tend to the horses. The two wondered if he ever spoke.

They seemed to be the only three in the inn.

When they were finished the child returned, and did speak to them, and they saw old old eyes in the young face.

"You have come to the Inn at the End of the World," he said. "You are welcome here, and should rest."

"And where else?" asked Elan. "I saw no other shelter in all this wild country."

"There is none. This Inn is the only lodging, and the last, in all the High Country. But you know that, or you would not have ventured here. No man enters the High Country save he comes on a quest. It is only when the cold bites and the darkness threatens that men seek the fire."

Both men nodded.

"Then you shall tell of your quest in the morning. Come now, and sleep. I have prepared a place for you." He led them upstairs to their beds.

~ three ~

The child with the wise eyes woke them for breakfast and left them to eat alone in silence. Afterwards the two ventured outside. Tall snowdrifts pressed against the sides of the Inn, and the long fangs of icicles dangled from the eaves. The air was cold, but had lost its bitter bite. They sat on the wide wooden step, freshly broomed from the covering that had fallen in the night.

"The snow has stopped, at least," said Elan.

"It nearly took your life, my young friend. You are lucky."

"No. I have a brave companion."

"I did not mean that. I only envy you the true peril of the cold." He stood. "It is warm beyond here - too warm?" He stepped away from the door and looked down past the stables, away from the white wastelands and the trackless paths that had carried them to the Inn. "Look, Elan - it is not winter everywhere!" Elan crept forward, and he too stared with startled eyes. Beyond the stables lay a valley, wrapped in the gold and crimson and orange of deep fall. A long row of tall tombstones lined the banks, reigning over mounds of earth and fallen leaves. And at the far end of the cleft they saw a Giant sitting on a giant stone. His back was to them, and beyond the rock and the Giant they saw ... nothing. Nothing but the nothingness of an immense void.

"Alabaster," the young man whispered, "we have truly come to the End of the World."

"It is the end anyway," came the murmured reply. "If we have not found our goal, or if refusal and disappointment lie in wait for us, there is no other place to turn. We have been all places in all lands and proved all other hopes hopeless."

Then the child spoke behind them. "Did you not seek this place? And that is He whom you must see, for in all places there must be a Master, and He is Master of all places. Let us go to Him."

Sudden fear fell upon them, yet they followed the child down out of the drifted snow and winter air into the crisper air of autumn and the banks of fallen leaves. The child walked slowly here, heedless of haste, as though time were not - and indeed it seemed that time too slumbered under the earth. Elan and Alabaster wondered at the strangeness of the High Country and viewed the high-standing gravestones. They read the name on the first marker silently. They looked at each other, then away, then moved on.

Halfway down the valley, Elan spoke. "Alabaster ... these graves. These names. These are all the old gods."

"I know. We have worshiped them all, and offered sacrifices in their names."

"Is it any wonder now that all our costly gifts were in vain?"

Their steps slowed even further, their weary feet turning to lead as they neared the end of the valley, the Giant on the stone, and the unfaced blackness beyond.

"Alabaster ... I am afraid," said Elan, in a whisper that rustled like the falling leaves.

"And I," returned Alabaster, under his breath. "This is not ground where men may walk unbidden."

The child turned to them. "Fear not," he said, "though you tread upon holy soil, for I am with you. Your guide is also your pledge, and your safety."

Then the long rows of graves were behind them and they stood together behind the Giant on the stone.

"Father," the child said, "they have come."

The Giant turned.

"Come," he commanded, in a rumble that rippled the rich earth beneath their feet. "Come, sit with me on the First Stone, and the Last, and know that you have reached the End of the World."

With no other choice, they obeyed freely, and turned their steps toward the stone. But the rock was smooth and immense and high, and offered them no foothold. The Giant reached down for them, and they stilled their racing hearts as the stupendous fingers curled around them and swept them up to the heights.

For a time they were aware only of the Giant, as those who first see the blazing stars in midnight stillness forget the earth beneath their feet. It seemed to them that the Giant and the stone were one, as though one had been carved from the other, and there was nothing between the two but a melding of the one into the other.

Then the Giant commanded them to look out into the void. Starless, it stunned them and spun their senses within them. Time ticked without measure before Alabaster found courage to murmur, as much to himself as to anyone, "It is not the sky."

The Giant answered him with soft thunder. "No. It is not the sky. The sky hangs over your head, and above all the path behind you, open to your sight if you turn your face to the heavens. But before you, Alabaster, do you see here the things you came seeking?"

"No. I see nothing."

"Nor you, Elan?"

"No ... sir."

"You call me sir? You do well. Perhaps you will yet call me Master."

"I perceive that we are known to you, for we have given our names to no one."

"Not given your names? Who gave those names to you?" The Giant laughed, and the valley behind threw back heartlifting echoes. "You have come to the Stone where all names are first named, and you wonder that I know you? You will find greater wonders yet."

He gestured to the blankness before them. "You see nothing here because I have not given you eyes to see forward. You see the heavens above, and the earth beneath, because they are, and have long been. But from this Stone forward are the things which have not yet come to pass. I call what comes, and brood over it, and ordain it, and my hand is always at work, shaping, molding, beckoning, creating. This is not the cold and empty abyss of nothing, but the warm darkness of the womb. It carries not the stillness of the dead, but the hush of things which are about to be born. I see now all these things that you cannot, secrets of which you cannot begin to conceive.

"It is not so much the End of the World, as its Beginning."

The Giant turned his eyes upon them, and they both blanched at the piercing of that brightness. "Your quests are known to me," he said, slowly, ponderously, as though thinking great thoughts at a great distance, "but you do not yet know the whole of each other's tale. And I desire to hear your own words from your own mouths. Share them now, and I will perhaps tell you what you do not know."

Alabaster closed his eyes. "I am Alabaster. I am more than nine hundred years old."

"You are nine hundred and ninety-nine years old, and ten months and fourteen days," said the Giant. "Soon your eyes will have seen a thousand years."

Alabaster turned his face to the abyss. "I no longer number the years. Even the decades pass without my noting. I simply *am* - and the centuries are a weariness unto death - a death that never comes. And that is my quest. To find death."

The Giant spoke again. "Many would conquer death."

"I do not seek to conquer. I seek to surrender to that which has knelt before me. Death has been no willing captor."

Elan asked, "How did you gain life unending, the gift that I covet? Are you more than a man?"

"Were I more than a mere man, would I have come this dark and weary way? No, I am mortal man stripped of mortality.

"I was once a king, and I destroyed a wizard - a wizard evil beyond measure. He cursed me as he died, screaming, 'I lay this upon you, that when your servant comes to you his first plea be granted!' His words puzzled me. And when I next ascended my throne, my servant came, and bowed low, and said, 'O king! May you live forever!'

"And so it was. A hundred years, and I died not, and then another hundred, without even an illness, and life became a burden unbearable. I sought the secret lair of the wizard I had slain - hoping he had left words of greater magic against such a time - but when I found his unholy nesting-place it was only shambles and ashes. I sought out other wizards - and had them boiled when they could not take my life with their powers. I challenged the sword of every warrior in the land, sending forth proclamations offering my throne to any who could slay me. I flung myself from every height onto the rocks and into icy waters. I tested the steel of my own blade - all in vain. I sought the basilisk under forgotten desert ruins - and saw only the ordinary ugliness of lizards. I bought for a terrible price the Gorgon's Head - but the curse she carried was a lesser one than my own.

"All in vain, all in vain. I have plumbed the depths of vanity and desperation, and found no cure.

"My kingdom prospered, and my reign was secure. My power grew and my warriors were many, for who would not fight for a king who could not die?

"In the end, after three hundred years, I vanished quietly from my own kingdom, like a thief stealing silently away in the night. I hoped that they would choose another king and exalt him, forgetting me, and that perhaps as their memory faded I too would fade, wither, and die. But it was not so. My empire has long since returned to sand - and I am still here. In vain have I used many mortal medicines and potent poisons, and nowhere is there an end for me.

"I should never have slain so great a wizard. A thousand years passing, and still his curse binds me. And he went laughing and cursing to his grave ..."

The Giant roused and spoke. "His powers of magic were born of the great darkness. You did rightly to kill him, and you did so by my hand, though you knew it not, for I despise sorcerers and abhor wizards and their familiars and potions and shifting wraps of shadows. You found his lair torn and his secret books burned - my servants doing my will destroyed his place of alchemy and fed his new and ancient papers to the flames. He had done evil enough, and it was not my choice that his knowledge pass to another. Not even to yourself, Alabaster, for you would not have found the curse's cure among his books. You would have found worse - the secrets and powers that corrupt, and corrupt absolutely. Better for you is life without end than life with unending power. His secrets would have made you a ceaseless horror. Had you not destroyed him, he would have subdued and twisted all the earth. Nor would the earth have endured you. And it will not endure the one who comes after, the one who gave birth to that wizard, the one who broods, cave-bound, over the destruction he will unleash, the very one who hates the workings of my hands and my servants' hands.

"The father is ever greater than the son, and that father is apace now, biding the ripe time to return. And the son was brought forth to undo the works of that ancient foe." He lifted his hands, and showed them on the face of the void a star blooming in a sable sky.

He lowered his hands, and the star vision faded.

"And you, Elan?" the Giant rumbled.

"I have no story such as Alabaster tells. I am only Elan, a youth - a suckling babe in the eyes of Alabaster. I savor the nectar of this flower called Life - I ask only that it never pass from me, never fade, never grow stale. My life is a pearl of great value. I am happy now, and sad only when I think of the coming darkness. Oh, that I might never change from these moments ..."

The Giant tilted his head. "He has seen your lifetime fifty times over, and grown weary of it. Is it now in your mind to ask that the curse be lifted from Alabaster and laid upon you instead?"

"It is," answered Elan bravely. "It is also said that the One Who Sits holds all powers in his hand - can you not transfer his curse as a blessing to me?"

"I am able. But I am unwilling to do so. There are other things more needful. And if I were to grant you your desire, you would not find it an unmixed blessing. You, too, would return here in a few centuries to this Rock and plead for the boon Alabaster now seeks."

After a silence, Alabaster asked, "Do you give us no hope, then?"

"You have not yet asked for hope. You have only asked for answers."

"You have given us no answers - so what hope is there?"

"I will give you a task, a quest, a mission. In fulfilling it you will face the truth, and when you have fulfilled it you may return and have your answer."

"You cannot answer us now?"

"You would not understand my answer. It would seem utter folly to you - yet, if you follow to its very end the task I give you, I give you my word that you shall hear my answer and find it good. He who seeks a gift from me may accept it only on my terms - but what I grant I grant freely."

"What, then, is this quest? I truly believe that we have already done every hard thing."

"There remains this. You have not ventured where I would send you because you have not believed the legends. And you could not journey there unless I send you with a seal of safety, a sign for your security, a secret that will save you.

"You must journey to the center of the earth, and find there the Secret Fire, and return to me each a double handful of its flame."

The two men stared at each other, reading fear in each other's eyes.

"You have not believed," said the Giant, "but it is so. Your wordsmiths wrote of it long ago - how the Secret Fire was sent to burn at the heart of the world. It burns still, and will never die; its fuel is love, its light is laughter, and its flame is joy. Is it not written that the heart of the earth is a star? And I have already shown you that star.

"You must go to the depths of the earth, where down is no more and all paths lead upward. There are many roads, but only one holy way. The many are easy, yet dark and deceiving, and their final end is death and destruction and despair. You have heard of these ways, and tested the first steps of those roads. Heed not those invitations." He traced his fingers in glowing streaks on the face of the abyss, and cast pictures there. "Through the marshes of the dead things, where cold lights wander, and past the forest of silence where dread things scream without sound, by the walls of forgotten cities where blue fire devours the unwary - this, and beyond, is your path."

Their blood slowed to a sluggish crawl in their veins, and their fear returned to them with unwelcome strength - not because such things were beyond their imagination, but because such horrors were fresh in their memories and very dark and monstrous indeed.

"These things we know of," said Alabaster faintly. "And well remembered is that path, though little loved. We have seen those dread places with our own eyes, and dared go no further, for we thought we had left sanity behind and come to the very edge of the perilous earth."

"You shall return, and pass through, and follow the paths beyond," promised the Giant, "paths in places where you thought there were no places. But you will not be overwhelmed. You shall journey through trackless mountains, but never lose your way, for I am with you, and that these things come to pass is the sign that I have sent you. There is a passage into the earth - long lost, seldom sought, hidden well. Enter and descend, speak my name, and the vigilant Flame will subside before you, will welcome you and not consume you.

"Bring me, each of you, a portion of that Secret Fire - and then I will answer you. But you must risk all on the way - you, Elan, must go unarmed, without sword or shield or knife. You, Alabaster, may carry the sword if you find steel necessary. You, and you alone, may fight."

Alabaster broke in. "This is folly! We go among thieves, madmen, and terrors! Give Elan the sword. I cannot be killed."

"My words do not work that way. You who would lose your life must strive to retain it. And you, who would find life everlasting, must be ever ready to throw it away.

"But you will venture forth with no ordinary blade. Give me your sword, Alabaster." Alabaster drew his sword and offered it to the Giant. The Giant brandished it like a carving knife and drew his fingers along the blade, striking sparks with his touch and leaving it a fiery red that faded as they watched. He returned the sword to Alabaster. "I have graven my word upon the edge, for it is ever sharper than steel. You may draw in times of peril, and in such times the mere sight of this word may deliver you. Be ready, but do not strike unless you must rescue Elan." He shifted on the stone and gazed down the autumn valley. "And now I must mark your hands before you may approach the Secret Fire." He bade them hold their palms out, and then touched the centers with one massive outstretched finger. Hot pain seared them, and they cried out, and then the agony passed, and each man found fresh old scars like dark healed holes in their hands.

"You bear now the Mark of the Child," the Giant said softly, "which I bear myself. For you, for now, these scars are your safety and will permit you passage through the forbidden places under the earth. Bring the Fire back in your hands, each of you, speedily, yet with care, for the Fire will quickly perish unless it returns to me.

"Go now with the Child, and sleep in the Inn tonight. You must leave tomorrow - this night is given you to choose your way, whether you will ride the paths I have made clear for you or whether you will return to the world of men and seek other answers. Remember that he who comes to the High Country must turn back, pass on, or perish. This is not a gentle region. You bring hard questions - you must expect hard answers and hard choices as well."

He sent them away with the Child and turned again to the abyss.

~ four ~

Troubled, Elan, tossed in his bed, pursuing sleep that would not surrender. Alabaster, too, stared at the darkness with unblinking eyes. They heard singing, elsewhere in the Inn, somewhere above or below or beside them.

I cannot hear the words, thought Alabaster. *Are they so far away, above the stars, or are they other tongues?*

I cannot hear them plainly, thought Elan. But he wept at the sound - high, far, lovely.

As they listened, their decisions crystallized with gentle force, easing their final hesitations, bringing light upon them like clouds drawing away from the face of the moon. They slept, and slept deeply, and dreamed of many wonders they could not carry with them into the waking world.

~ five ~

The Child woke them, and after a meal they all stepped out the door of the Inn.

Their horses stood saddled, pawing the ground with rested restlessness.

The Giant stood quietly and immovable beyond the horses, a still point in the turning universe, as though the solid world itself had parted for his passing and closed in behind him.

"You will go, then?" asked the Giant, his soft words rumbling the earth beneath them.

"We will go," answered Alabaster.

"Have you set aside your doubts and your fears?"

"No," said Elan, "but we go anyway."

The Giant nodded. "Then you do well, and you will do well."

"It is time," added Alabaster. "We have found rest here, but another night would not prepare us further."

"Time means little here," said the Giant, "and either you are ready or you are not.

"One more thing is needful," he continued, "or you venture vainly."

And he told them his three Names, and each one was more terrible and strong than the one before it. The trees in the valley shook down their golden burdens at the sound, and the power of the named Names trembled the frozen earth.

"Do not utter them," warned the Giant, "save in your gravest need. And then do not hesitate to utter them, even the High Name, for they will deliver you when all other names are dead and powerless and empty vanity, mere noises in the wind."

Still stunned, their minds reeling, both men swung themselves into their saddles. When they looked up again the Giant was gone, and only the Child stood there.

The morning light haloed the Child as he watched the two travelers ride away into the snowy wasteland, and when they were mere suggestions on the horizon of his eyes he blessed them again.

Then the Child tended to the Inn, and to the needs of the few and desperate wayfarers at odd times after, and often he would pass through the valley of the fallen gods to lean against the Giant's shoulder and watch the swirling of the void.

~ six ~

Alabaster and Elan found their way perilous, beyond their fears and beyond their ability to endure, save that the hollow hunger in their hearts drove them on.

At every turn they found their passage opposed. At first their enemies were only human; their track led them down into forgotten valleys where lived those men who cared not for guests, but welcomed questers only as prey.

There came a day when they ceased to hope for hospitality, and a later day when they abandoned hope of any help from any people they might encounter on their way.

And as they drew further into the wilderness, farther from even the memory of the civilizations left behind them, they were faced by men who hardly seemed men any longer.

"Alabaster," said Elan, "we have passed from the world of men into the realm of the beasts - but I confess I do not know where we crossed that border."

"Nor do I," replied Alabaster grimly. "Not all borders are well-marked for the traveler.

"But they are not beasts - they are worse, for beasts would only seek us for food or strike to protect their own kind. And these - men - seek our lives only in unreasoning evil."

"We are alone, Alabaster - well and truly alone," Elan declared at last.

"Perhaps," said the ancient traveler. "I have found that when strong memories linger you are never truly alone." He thought of the Child and the Giant, and knew that Elan's thoughts ran beside his own.

And then after many days they began to encounter fell beasts that were beasts in truth and nature, and after that appeared dread shadows that seemed to them like demons.

Alabaster's sword flashed often, and some fell back at the sight of the runes on the blade, while only the edge of the sword prevailed against others, and Alabaster stooped in the silence of victory to wipe the gore from the shining steel. Some of the mightier foes pressed the fight until Elan spoke the First Name, and even some strong shadows persevered until he gave voice to the Second Name.

There were other dangers of which they had no knowledge, and for which they had no names. Blue lights flared in the darkness, blue lights that would have drawn them aside with dark luring, had their faces not been set like stone towards a different, and unknown, destination. They heard soft voices, almost human, that bade them turn aside, but they pressed on.

But all their foes gave way at last, and Elan brooded long over the power that lay in their grasp. "Alabaster, we could not have journeyed here, even if we had dared. This has long been your sword, but without the Giant's marks, and without the Names of Power, we would have been defeated and destroyed long since."

Alabaster nodded grimly, and added nothing to his words.

Then the last of the earth they knew fell behind them, and they came to the edge of a vast wasteland. They reined in their mounts and stared at the dead, cold, lifeless expanse before them, devoid of all comforting features and empty of any promise.

"We have defeated all our foes," said Alabaster. "From now on, the way itself will be our enemy."

"Where is this cave, then?" asked Elan angrily. "Where is this passage to the heart of the earth? We have stood at the end of the world already, and surely now we have come to the other side, with nothing beyond it."

But Alabaster was silent in his patience, and led them into the wasteland, seeing no path, hoping for none, but only looking for a way deeper into the wilderness.

The desert swallowed them, and they rode in silence over the frozen sand and scoured rock.

The sun faded into a pale orb as they passed beyond its reach into the depths of a permanent winter. Snow fell thickly upon them, and deep drifts crept stealthily to block their way and hinder them, and long icicles grew like glittering daggers from their cloaks and saddles.

"We shall freeze before we find the way to the Heart of the Earth," Elan mumbled through lips stiffened with the relentless cold.

"Yes - we are cold indeed," returned Alabaster, "and so it shall be all the easier to find the heat - and it shall be all the more welcome when we find it."

~ seven ~

They sensed their goal long before they saw it.

"Fires burn somewhere," Elan said. "I feel the heat of the flames, though I see nothing."

"We shall see it soon enough," returned Alabaster. "We need only keep our face to the warmth, and our path will find itself under our feet."

The horses sensed it too, and found new speed to urge their tired legs forward. They labored on, and rode up into a low range of swelling hills. Before them the air began to shimmer, and the snow dwindled, and once more there was only rock beneath them.

They crested a long rise, and stopped.

We are here, they both thought.

What lay before them was no cave, with no easy sloping floor, but a vast crater in the earth like the navel of the world, a narrow way spiraling down the rim into unguessable lightless depths.

A band of green like a garden circled the funnel, and its bright life smote their weary eyes.

"There is grass here," observed Elan finally, "and flowers, but no trees."

"The snow gives way to water," Alabaster said, pointing out the thin trickles that wound their way out of the wilderness and felt their way into the caverns below. "Where there is warmth there is life."

They urged their mounts on, and let them graze long on the abundant grass while the two men dismounted to drink their fill of the fresh water, bask in the baking heat, and gaze without speaking at the next stage of their journey.

"We have no torches," said Elan. "There is little here to burn, and what is here is too green."

"Let us go as far as we may," his companion said. "It may be that torches will not be our greatest need."

"Yes. We have seen many strange things already. Another wonder would be no surprise - and perhaps our steps will take us to a place that holds no darkness."

But their horses would not set foot on the final path, so Elan and Alabaster lightened their own packs as far as they dared and turned toward the winding way.

"We need not hobble them," Elan observed. "They have no place to go."

"Let us leave our cloaks here as well," replied Alabaster. "We shall not need them until we return."

Elan tried not to think of the unguarded drop that lay beside them as they ventured down the spiral path. *My life has been too short,* he thought, *but those last few seconds would be far too long.*

Alabaster eyed the edge warily as well, thinking not of death but of lying broken and helpless on whatever bottom he might find. *There would be no end down there - only suffering with no release.*

Yet they went on with care and watchfulness, and long, long they descended, until the dim daylight was only a pale memory high above them.

At last Alabaster stopped. "We can go no further," he said. "The way is too treacherous without light."

"Look to your sword," said Elan, behind him. "I think your scabbard hides the deeper truth from us."

Alabaster drew, and the blade flared forth in the gloom, and lit enough of their path to set their feet in confidence.

"And so the Giant has provided, and we knew it not." He brandished the sword before them. "See - the light comes from the runes he left in the steel."

"All his words have proven true - so far. Let us see what lies ahead."

The heat grew and drew beads of sweat on their brows, and them baked them dry again. Hours passed, and they paused to eat sparingly from their packs, drinking from the water that still tumbled at odd points beside the path.

After a second rest, and a third, and a fourth, they came to a parting of the path. A vast lake glimmered in the glow of the sword, and they saw that they had come to an end of their direct descent. Before them the path vanished into an opening, a mere hole in the enormous expanses of the ancient rock.

They drank deeply, and filled their worn waterskins, not knowing when they would see fit water again. Then they entered the beckoning cavern without a word.

~ eight ~

Almost immediately, the tunnel divided and left them adrift in uncertainty.

"Which way do we turn? whispered Elan. "All these paths seem the same. And all go down."

Alabaster held his sword higher aloft. "I would have chosen *this* way," he said, "but look you at the blade. It grows brighter when I cast its light upon *this* path."

Elan pointed to the darker path. "Walk there, a pace or two."

Alabaster did, and the sword dimmed to a threadlike glow.

"Come back."

Alabaster returned to the chosen path, and the sword brightened once again in his hand. They followed the ceaseless shining down, and again to the next parting of the paths, and the next, until they knew they were hopelessly lost without their guide.

"Do not drop it," murmured Elan, "though your arm grow weary, or we are dead men."

"You perhaps, would be lost for a time, and soon dead. I would only be lost forever. Which would be the lesser fate?"

"The Giant said that none could come here without his leave. Perhaps that is so - but none could ever leave without aid such as this."

They persevered, and rested, and on what was perhaps the second or third day they sensed a change ahead. Somewhere before them there was sound, and a faint glow that ebbed and faded even as they tried to discern it.

The way dipped and twisted one final time, and led them out into a great arching hall. They stopped, afraid and dazzled by sudden sound and light.

An incredible song of fire pulsed in the tunnels and haunted the heartbeat of the hidden earth - flame and heat and light and music and boundless energy. Irresistible, it roared and challenged them, and held them back, and they were afraid until Alabaster remembered to speak the Giant's third and secret Name. That Name echoed in every recess around them, and then the unendurable flare of the fire became durable laughter, and kindled sudden joy in their hearts.

The rocks were not hot, though the air shimmered with waves of unseen fire and heat hammered at their faces. The source was the great radiant Being before them, and not the earth itself.

That Being was liquid fire and roiled through the smoking tunnels beneath the earth. There were no shadows, and no possibility of shadows, for the light was everywhere and shone in all directions.

The fire was before them and behind them and beside them. There was no escape, nor did they wish to find their way out.

Long they gazed, and marveled, and pleasured in the warmth, until at last they remembered their mission.

"How can we carry this back? We have only our hands."

"Then we must use them."

They reached out together, hesitating for only one final heartbeat, and plunged their hands into the liquid light.

Alabaster grasped for the fire, but could not hold it.

Elan scooped the restless flames, but the fire seeped through his fingers. *It's alive,* he thought. *We cannot carry this back with mortal hands.*

How do we carry this back? he thought. *I cannot hold this in my hands, or grasp it ...*

But the fire they sought to handle sank into the holes in their hands, and left them with nothing but its memory in their fingers.

It is toying with us, he thought. *It could consume us in a heartbeat - yet it has not, and I do not fear that it shall.*

Then the fire around them became the fire within them, and they felt the burning of the Child's marks on their hands, and the flames brought them the healing inner warmth they had long longed for and all but given up as a hopeless dream. Their bones were warmed, and their hearts were cheered, and old chills they had forgotten they carried were banished forever.

The fire brought its own knowledge with it, and they felt the light and knew it for the same fire that brought upon them the glowing rays of the day and watched over them in the cold nights from the stars. It was all one, and they stood helpless but unharmed in the power of the sun.

There is a fire that burns at the heart of the earth ...

They beheld the fire, and could see nothing except the flames; they felt it, and breathed it deep within their bodies, and heard nothing but its ceaseless singing.

And then the flames ebbed as they had come, leaving them alone yet no longer desolate in the long and winding ways beneath the earth. The fire withdrew with a tender finality, and they knew they would not see it again.

"We must go back," said Alabaster, after a long and dazed silence. "We are finished here, though we have failed. Our hearts are full, but our hands are empty."

Elan nodded mutely, pausing long before saying, "Let us go back - and then throw ourselves upon the Giant's mercy. Surely he will know how hopeless was the task he set us - for how could anyone seize hold of this great fiery spirit and carry it away in his hands?"

"We are privileged, though we have failed," whispered Elan. "Who can come here without its leave? And who can leave here without its warmth?"

"We are alone now," Alabaster agreed, "but will *this* ever be far away? He burns beneath the earth in all places everywhere, and so at all times he will be under our feet."

"If this be the same fire that flames the sun and candles the stars, then he will never be far away. He must always be over our head, or wrapping us in his light."

"And within our memories, and within our hearts. Nevertheless, we must go. We were sent, and now we must return by that same summons."

The light of the sword led them back up the long and winding way, though its light seemed pale and wan against the memory of the Secret Fire.

I value its guidance, thought Alabaster, *but I might have known the way now without it.*

Everything is different now, thought Elan. *I scarcely know what I still know.*

The two men climbed at last to the rim of the giant crater, looking down and back at the warm darkness and then out at the frozen wasteland.

"The way back is no shorter than the path that led us here," said Elan. "Yet somehow I am no longer afraid."

"We came on a quest with a shrouded end," replied Alabaster, "and we return to a destination we know all too well. We came with faint hopes, and impoverished imaginations - and now we return with fiery certainties, and knowledge that cannot be dimmed. Let us ride boldly, and fear nothing, and let all who would oppose us look to their own safety."

They both smiled as they groomed the waiting, well-grazed horses and saddled them again for the long ride.

~ nine ~

The stars shifted overhead, slowly, nightly, and the pale moon waned and waxed and waned again, and each night and each morning the Child stood before the Inn and gazed calmly into the distance.

But there was an end to his patient vigil, and at last there came the night when the Child threw wide the door and held lanterns high to welcome the two travelers a second time.

~ ten ~

"You may approach him without my guidance," said the Child. "Free you are to venture on your own, for I am already with you, though you know it not." Elan and Alabaster gladly abandoned their dust-stained packs; turning aside the thoughts of rest, they straightaway turned their troubled steps down the valley, passing with empty hands the long gauntlet of upright graven stones.

"You have gone safely, and returned," the watching Giant rumbled above their heads. "Did not my words prove true?"

"Yes. Your name was on the sword - but your Name, not the sword - broke every barrier and subdued every threat. And your Secret Name opened the final path into the Fire. And still we marvel at the peril of the way."

"And you have returned - and so it is time to claim my due."

The two questers stared at the ground.

I held it for an instant, thought Elan, *and one instant only. Through the marks. I could feel the heat there, as I feel it now. I have failed. I am ashamed, but no longer afraid.*

And Alabaster. *There is nothing left to give you. It all runs in our veins. We have failed. Why do I not despair? Somehow I think you knew this would happen.*

Our hearts were refined with its fire, they both thought. *It lifted us up, and burned old dross and left only a furnace inside our hearts that was like the furnace inside the earth.*

"You have come empty-handed?" asked the Giant. "But not empty! Look behind you!" He pointed a massive hand, and the earth shifted. They looked, and their footprints glowed behind them and their own bright shadows shone upon the leafy ground. "You leave the Mark of the Secret Fire wherever you walk! And because you bear that within you I know that you are not discouraged."

They looked at each other. "No," said Elan. "I am ..."

"We are ... at peace," finished Alabaster.

"And if I bade you forsake your quests, would you do so?"

"Yes," they both answered, softly, but without uncertainty, and surprised by their own words.

"Those things don't seem to matter so much now," Alabaster confessed.

"Somehow we have ... changed," added Elan.

The Giant nodded, and somewhere an empire toppled. "Such is the way of the Secret Fire. From its first touch you were changed, but slowly, and you saw it not, for darkness has veiled your eyes all your lives, and you did not know what it was like to see.

"I bade you bring me two portions of the Fire - yet you have not fully delivered them into my hands. I am the Lord of the Secret Fire, and I call now for what is mine. And that which is mine is that which you once called yours. Come - I claim *you*."

And they knew they had no choice, for the Fire was in them now and thus made them his. They offered themselves, and the Giant wrapped giant hands around them and once again lifted them up beside him on the rock.

"You are mine now, as you have always been, and I am yours, as I long might have been. Never will you regret this surrender.

"Drink this." He offered them a golden cup, and they marveled, for it was the cup of which all other glorious goblets are only a pale shadow. But they obeyed and took it in their hands, and beheld the blood-red wine surging in its depths. "It is new wine - but the finest. It is my own vintage, and I have withheld the best until the last." They drank, and the draught burned inside them, as though the Secret Fire and the wine had mingled in a dance of joy.

Then their eyes were opened, and hidden wisdom long planted in their hearts flowed full. They understood many dazzling things then that had long been dark and shrouded mysteries.

"And you shall understand more," the Giant continued. "You are mine now, and I yours, and you shall have my eyes to see and my ears to hear and my strong right arm to act. You have heard, obeyed, and surrendered. Listen now to the revealed wisdom of the ages, to the secrets of all the earth - and hear the fulfillment of your quests."

He directed their gazes down the valley. "There was a time," he said, "when men were permitted to raise vain shadows and call them gods. Those shadows were among the first signs of the coming darkness that must come before the final light. Do you see that the sun wanes and here is pale as the moon? Its flame is fleeing and soon will be flown. Darkness has come to cover the world, though men know it not, for its truth is seen only here at the End of the World. Dark it is already; darker still it will grow, to shroud all the earth in shadow - until the time comes for the Child to shine forth. He has come already, but is not yet manifest. And his flame shall shatter the darkness and outcandle the sun, and wax without end until the brightest light of the heavens is a memory and pale-orbed in the light of his eyes."

Then suddenly the Child appeared beside them on the rock and spoke with them. "I tend the Inn now, where winter dwells, for I was born in the winter of man." He held out his hands, and they saw the scars.

Elan said, "They are very like the scars we bear in your name."

"These are not scars - not as you reckon such. The marks upon your hands are the reminders of old wounds past. These that I bear are a foreshadow, the marks of wounds I have not yet received. Even so, your scars are echoes of my own."

He looked up, and his eyes tore them with pain-ridden knowledge. "For these and with these I was born. I will go into the world of men to receive them, and then when I have been wounded by the hands of men I will return here and sleep beneath this rock. But I will not sleep as these shadow gods sleep - for my Father will come and name this rock Rolled Away, and it shall be, and where the old gods sleep I shall come forth alone."

"These are wondrous things," the Giant said, "and men have not heard them clearly before. But you are prepared, for you have held the heart of the Elder God in your hands. We shall speak of them again.

"And now to your own quests.

"Alabaster. You did not seek immortality, but hold that it rests upon you as a curse. I tell you that you have always been immortal, and were created so - you might as well hope to hurl yourself headlong among the stars as to bring your existence to an end.

"These gods sleep forever, because they lived only as phantoms, the illusive creations of those who are themselves creations. Men who die do not sleep forever, but rise at my word and pass on to judgment and to other worlds which also lie in the palm of my hand.

"And you, Elan. Foolish is the man who will not accept that his life on earth is but a candle-flicker, and will fly like the flame of the waning sun. Many have sought to avoid the embrace of death; none have succeeded, save at my hand, for all must sleep that sleep of darkness before they come to this rock, which is my throne through all eternity.

"Your quests are fruitless - except that you have come to me. The works of sorcery may not be undone except by my magic, and the laws that govern the earth cannot be set aside except by my word. There is, however, an answer for each of you, a single draught to quench your separate thirsts.

"I have need of messengers to go to and fro upon the earth, to do my bidding and tell of the things I desire to be known. By such hands was the work of that wizard destroyed, and by such voices have the existence of the Secret Fire and the Inn been made known to all who listen for wise whispers.

"You shall be my messengers. I offer that to you, and bestow it upon you, and require it of you.

"It is death, in many ways, but you, Elan, will find it rest everlasting. It is a life above death, and a death better than life. None shall ever take your new life from you.

"All names are named here, and given meaning. Do you know the meaning of your name, Elan?"

"It means Seeker Under the Sun," the young man answered.

"That is its second meaning. Its first meaning is Life - and you shall bring the Life you have found to many. And you, Alabaster?"

"He who endures, as the stone itself," replied the ancient warrior.

"You, too, know only the second meaning. Its first is Vessel of the Gods. And you shall be no more an empty vessel of many phantom gods, but an overflowing vessel of the One God Who Reigns. You have seen one millennium, and shall see more, but the years behind will seem only a cast-off weariness, an abandoned burden, and the years to come will not grieve you, for nothing which has happened to you or will happen to you shall ever prevent you from casting aside the woeful weight of your old life."

Then he spoke a mighty word of power, and the earth trembled, and the ground beside the base of the rock burst open and a fountain of fire spewed high into the heavens. "Behold! The Secret Fire! The Fire That Was Sent to Burn at the Heart of the World! He comes at my bidding - he comes to make you clean - he comes to make you my chosen messengers - he comes to guide you from this day forward. Bathe! Dive deep into the laughter that heals and the zeal that cleanses!" He took the two in his hands and set them deep into the Fire, and the Child stood with them in the surging fires of the terrecelestial furnace, and they were not alone. The singing they had heard in the Inn and at the earth's core flowered full above and within them. In the hot caress of the flame they felt their old and weary beings melt and flow away like slag.

The Giant spoke again, and clapped his hands, and the Fire sank once more beneath the earth and left the four standing alone and newly together.

The two travelers stared at the Giant. "Yet ... if the Fire was *here,* at your command," said Alabaster, "why, then, did we journey?"

"The easy way would not have been hard enough for you, because you have long disdained the simple ways. Had you come to me first, seeking simply, your path would have been simple.

"That is why I said there is one path, or none. You, however, would not have grown wise on a short journey. Did you not change as you went? Even your very vision? Did not your coming differ from your going?"

Yes, thought Elan. *If a star has a face, we beheld it, and feared ... it looked so much like this Giant and this Child. And I shall never again see the world as I did.*

Yes, thought Alabaster, *we did not need the sword as we returned. Bearing the Fire, being burned by it, being filled with it, we saw the horrors in our path for what they were, and we passed without fear. The Fire gave us eyes, made us wise, made our steps secure.*

The Giant turned their faces toward the abyss. "The Secret Fire works slowly often, with hearts like yours, but then exceedingly deep. That is why I sent you on a hard road. You have proven your worth as my messengers." With another word and a wave of his hand he showed them out of the darkness things that were to come, terrible things, bright things, holy things - all that he desired the men of earth to come to know, and the Child was in the midst of them all.

"Do you desire to see more? He who finds knowledge finds life - but he may also find sorrow."

"Show us no more!" exclaimed Alabaster, "for we are only mortal!"

"Yet," added Elan, "show us all that pleases you, and we will watch and see these things."

He showed them yet more in their reluctance and their longing, and they were prostrate with fear and uplifted with hope confirmed. He showed them the steps and words and deeds of their first servants' journey, closed the face of the void before them, blessed them, and sent them to the Inn to rest.

~ eleven ~

Full of words, exhilarated and yet somber and set for the weary way ahead, Elan and Alabaster rode slowly away through the snow toward the pale morning sun. The door of the ancient Inn opened, and the Child came forth alone. He watched them go, and then turned to eye the wind in the valley as it flurried fallen leaves over the graves of the old gods.

###

afterword

Those who have read this far may wish to know more about the individual stories.

Regarding THE LAST OF THE WINE:

Even in spiritual darkness, the world has never lacked gods: wherever knowledge of the True God was lost or abandoned, men freely made gods to suit their hopes and needs and deepest fears. And man the creator did give an illusion of life to even the false gods. But that illusion could not last, and there came a moment when the vanity was exposed for all time. This short tale - the oldest story in this book - was originally written as a play, partially in response to a late night discussion about the hidden impact of the "hinge of history" - the Incarnation. It has been so performed on a few occasions, including by a group of my wife's third-grade students studying the triumphs and failures of ancient Greece and Rome.

Regarding A CURE FOR UNICORN:

No one can read and enjoy fantasy without cultivating a love for unicorns - those wondrous beasts who are too old and wild and strong even for man's imagination. Unicorns are irresistible; they are not only lovely, but lonely. I began to speculate about such an attractive being as a cure for loneliness - even a cure for the loneliness it causes - and this story evolved from there.

There are many echoes from John 14-17 here, though even I did not spot them all until the story was finished.

Regarding SHADOWBOX:

We all have our shameful secrets, and we all wish to keep our shame a secret. The paradox is that forgiveness, though freely offered, may only be effectively received when we surrender both our shame and our right to conceal our painful secrets.

A later and different treatment of this surfaced in chapter 13 of *The Chameleon Lady*, and there is also an abandoned place of worship standing in mute witness in *The Everlasting Child*.

Regarding CAPTAIN SUNSHINE AND THE RIGHT BROTHERS:

I have long been fascinated with the history of flight, and have appreciated the work and accomplishments of the Wright Brothers. And I have met people over the years who could have carried the name "Right Brothers" - applied not in praise but in derision, in recognition of their specific stupidity and apparently incurable narrow-mindedness.

This story was easy to think up, but hard to write. Cranking out a few sentences without punctuation (other than periods) was difficult enough; accomplishing the feat for a whole story gave me brain cramps. But that tone seemed to fit the story line well, so I stayed with it. (Neil Diamond fans will recognize a portion of the title and some of the images.) Though I did not notice it until long after the fact, the story resembles Eustace's early journals in *The Voyage of the Dawn Treader*.

There may also be some influence from an old issue of HIS Magazine - especially the illustrations that accompanied an article on "Self-Sufficient Airways." One might also speculate profitably on the influence of the original version of the film *The Flight of the Phoenix*.

Regarding HENDERSON'S LION:

This was written in a few days' span as an analogue for a jumble of Scripture verses, and "performed" for an adult Sunday school class as a discussion starter.

"... make no provision for the flesh, to gratify its desires ... but take every thought captive to obey Christ, being ready to punish every disobedience ... each person is tempted when he is lured and enticed by his own desire. Then desire when it has conceived gives birth to sin, and sin when it is full-grown brings death. Do not be deceived ..." (A conflation of Romans 13:14, II Corinthians 10:5-6, and James 1:14-16)

The discussion covered, in part, the regrettable tendency of the Christian community to give special attention to converts who are able to relate dramatic testimonies of depravity and rescue and salvation. More than a few of us wondered why we don't give equal attention to those wiser people who watched for and avoided the worst temptations along their way.

This is the closest thing in these stories to a straight parable. And there is more than a trace here of the Lions of Szavo.

Regarding CONCRETE AND THE SEA:

Delaine Peffley was a sweet and much-loved member of our college Christian fellowship. She graduated a year or two after I did, and moved on to work in South Bend, Indiana. I was sitting in our church service in Indianapolis when our mutual friend the pastor announced that Delaine had been killed that weekend in a car accident. Many of us knew her well, and cried, and questioned; several of us attended her funeral, and saw her buried, but we did not forget her.

I wrote this story soon after, trying to imagine what the sudden translation had been like for her.

Regarding THE LADY AND THE TIGER:

I love tigers. I have held fuzzy striped cubs in my arms, thrown meat to the grown ones, and watched them all for hours at the zoo and the animal rescue center. I have my share of horrid nightmares - but none of the bad dreams have tigers in them. Ever. Any dream with a tiger is a good one.

This story was written down in a single breathless and tear-stained scribble after a particularly lovely dream in the small hours of the night.

Regarding THROUGH THE GLASS DARKLY:

This story, on the other hand, came from a tigerless dream that was the essence of nightmare - a nightmare fueled, like so many others, by chronic depression - the modern word for the dark malady the ancients called *melancholy*. Depression is all darkness, and fear, and withdrawal into hiding (of various sorts) to avoid being hated and rejected for the inescapable flaws and unending failures. But the surprise of love is that one can be thoroughly known and be desired anyway.

A friend recently observed that the shadowed and shrouded Town here bears considerable resemblance to the Grey Town in *The Great Divorce* by C. S. Lewis. And it is Lewis who so ably suggested that the door of Hell is locked from the inside.

Regarding FOOLS' FOREST:

This was the last story in this collection to be plotted and written. The germ of the tale was jotted down long ago, with a few general notes about the resolution, but nothing was done until it was needed for this collection.

This story approaches allegory in places; there are conscious echoes of the wondrous but nearly-forgotten doctrines of the Descent into Hell (still mentioned and recited in the Apostles' Creed) and the medieval mystery play *The Harrowing of Hell*.

It is also an exploration of the question - "How do all the princesses and fair maidens wind up locked in lonely towers in the first place?"

Regarding THE TREASURE OF GALLOWS HOUSE:

No story here took longer to finish than this one. The outline was created more than twenty-five years ago; the beginning was drafted soon after, yet it lay dormant (like the fallow land) until the rest of these stories had been gathered and completed and were waiting patiently for it to join them.

Great houses and castles have always loomed large in my imagination, and this was an outgrowth of an insight into "not seeing the forest for the trees."

I haven't quite decided what this story means. It unfolded gradually as I wrote it, and was not fully envisioned beforehand. (The setting and the challenge were all that initially appeared in my imagination.)

It wasn't so planned (by me, anyway), but I suspect it is a metaphor for the Kingdom of God - and the fatal temptation of seeking the things of the Kingdom before seeking the Kingdom itself.

I think it also likely illustrates the proper attitude of those blessed Kingdom-finders who immediately begin sharing the good things they are allowed to find, inherit, claim, and enjoy.

Regarding THE FATE OF THE MOOR-WITCH,
TEETH IN THE NIGHT,
and THE WHEEL OF THE SKY:

Whenever I pass through Wheaton, I try to spend time with Jerry and Claudia Root. On one visit, they provided me with not only a room for the night but a black cat (Scrubb - named for Eustace, of course) to keep me warm. Jerry, a C. S. Lewis scholar and literary enthusiast, discovered my affection for cats and later presented me with an Arthur Rackham print depicting a scruffy black cat rubbing the ankles of a disreputable old witch on a windswept moor. On the solitary (and solitudinous) drive back to Indianapolis, I mentally composed most of "The Fate of the Moor-Witch." A special edition of that story (with a color reproduction of the Rackham print) was prepared for the Roots, and for friends who had given special support to my writing attempts.

When I next returned to Wheaton, and stayed with my hosts again, I wound up taking a night stroll with Claudia and their dog Dudley. I soon discovered that Dudley (a small, brown, inoffensive, beaglish-bassett hound) thought he was the fiercest beast in the village, the equal of anything on four legs, and the undisputed ruler of the darkness. He provided us all with great amusement; "Teeth in the Night" came naturally from that episode.

"The Wheel of the Sky" was written because I believe good stories come in threes, because Scrubb and Dudh Leye deserved a chance to combine their talents, and because a friend pointed out to me that both the witch and the farmer had a weighty responsibility to reach out to their neighbors with the knowledge that had been entrusted to them. (Strangely enough, in a book filled with names and meanings of names - and even names of names - I never discovered the names of the farmer and the white-haired woman. Like the two talking beasts, these people seem to have kept their own secrets.)

This is also an exploration of the gospel as *good news* - which will only be attractive and meaningful if the *bad* news has been proclaimed and accepted first. The whole message may be simple to declare, but often difficult to share effectively - for the scarcely believable may be rejected as the unbelievable.

The reader may also suspect (and rightly so) that I paid attention in Sunday school to the story of Lot and his family's flight from the doomed cities of Sodom and Gomorrah.

The idea of the comet likely sprang from "global disaster from space" movies of recent years, and most certainly from conscious consideration of the tales of theTunguskan meteor explosion of 1908; ironically, just after this long-neglected story was finally completed, another meteorite exploded over Russia. I was also thinking of the celestial wonder that was seen as the Star of Bethlehem - a sign of peace ... but what if another wonder had come bearing a different message?

And yes, anyone with a good imagination might well hear a specific *Journey* song playing at considerable volume in the background.

Regarding A CHILD OF THE SNOWS
and THE INN AT THE END OF THE WORLD:

"A Child of the Snows," of course, is not my own poem but Chesterton's. It is a magnificent flight of the imagination, and both sparked and fit perfectly with my ponderings of the deaths of the old and false pagan gods. I have a hard time appreciating poetry (which undoubtedly says more about me than the poems), but Chesterton's work has always appealed to me - an irresistible rolling rhythm with a wealth of wondrous words and indelible images. "A Child of the Snows" has long been one of my favorites, and we used it as a family Christmas card one year.

"The Inn at the End of the World" was written largely on the strength of Chesterton's poem, and deliberately embodies many of his images and phrases. There is also a strong taste of the Wandering Jew legend, with a sampling of my own life and hopes, disappointments and triumphs, and moments of weariness and exultation.

The original drafts went in quite different directions from the final version; the vast hole in the distant earth where the travelers eventually descend was a tower in the ancient and preliminary notes - the ruins, to be precise, of something very much like the Tower of Babel. Such a Tower was intriguing imagery, and I was reluctant to set it aside, but in the end I was convinced it did not fit with the final shape of the story. Instead of climbing towards the heavens in the arrogant footsteps of the first builders, it was more meaningful that Alabaster and Elan should burrow their way deep into the earth in claustrophobic humility to discover the roiling Fire at its heart.

There are knowing and deliberate echoes from J. R. R. Tolkien, William Hope Hodgson, the Moody Blues, and other writers and artists who have touched upon our primal fears and deepest hopes - whether or not they glimpsed the final answers.

This tale was planned from the first as a brief but vivid bookend to this collection; however, it grew exponentially in the act of writing to claim the title of the largest, richest, and most intricate story in the book. It was definitely the most intoxicating to invent and shape and record, for Chesterton's imagination fired mine with its sweep and grandeur. In some ways, I feel that the best was saved for the last.

The artwork on the cover is a detail from a larger painting by my daughter, Jennifer. My stories sparked her imagination, and she was able to capture her vision of the High Country and the Inn for me as a special birthday gift.

www.ingramcontent.com/pod-product-compliance
Lightning Source LLC
Chambersburg PA
CBHW050403110726
47899CB00008B/2627